Killing Bridezilla

Books by Laura Levine

THIS PEN FOR HIRE

LAST WRITES

KILLER BLONDE

SHOES TO DIE FOR

THE PMS MURDER

DEATH BY PANTYHOSE

KILLING BRIDEZILLA

Published by Kensington Publishing Corporation

A Jaine Austen Mystery

Killing Bridezilla

Laura Levine

KENSINGTON BOOKS
http://www.kensingtonbooks.com

KENSINGTON BOOKS are published by

Kensington Publishing Corp.
850 Third Avenue
New York, NY 10022

All Kensington titles, imprints, and distributed lines are available at special quantity discounts for bulk purchases for sales promotion, premiums, fund-raising, educational, or institutional use.

Special book excerpts or customized printings can also be created to fit specific needs. For details, write or phone the office of the Kensington Special Sales Manager: Attn. Special Sales Department. Kensington Publishing Corp., 850 Third Avenue, New York, NY 10022. Phone: 1-800-221-2647.

Kensington and the K logo Reg. U.S. Pat. & TM Off.

Library of Congress Card Catalogue Number: 2008923400

ISBN-13: 978-0-7582-2043-1
ISBN-10: 0-7582-2043-X

First Printing: June 2008
10 9 8 7 6 5 4 3 2 1

Printed in the United States of America

For Mark

Acknowledgments

Many thanks, as always, to my editor John Scognamiglio for his unwavering faith in me and Jaine, and to my agent Evan Marshall for his valued guidance and support. Thanks also to Hiro Kimura, whose nifty covers never fail to bring a smile to my face. And to Joanne Fluke, who takes time out from writing her own bestselling Hannah Swensen mysteries to share her insights and her brownies. To Mark Baker, for being there from the beginning. And to R. T. Jordan, because he is a good friend, and because I want to plug his Polly Pepper mysteries.

A special thanks to the wonderful readers who've taken the time to write me. And to my friends and family for putting up with me while I'm wrangling with a plot. Finally, a loving thanks to my most loyal fan and ardent supporter, my husband Mark.

Chapter 1

Some people look back on their high school days fondly, lost in happy memories of pep rallies and senior proms. And then there are the other 98% of us. For us, high school was hell with acne, a blistering nook of inferno Dante neglected to mention, where we first discovered that life isn't fair and blondes really do have more fun.

Which is why I cringed when I first got that call from Patti Marshall. In the Dante-esque world of high school, Patti was Satan's ringmaster.

But I'm getting ahead of myself. Let me back up and set the scene.

I'd just come home from the vet, where I'd taken my cat Prozac for her annual checkup. You'll be happy to learn Prozac was in perfect health. The vet, however, required several stitches and a trip to the emergency room.

"How could you attack poor Dr. Graham like that?" I scolded as I let her out of her cage.

I warned her to stay away from my privates.

"I still can't believe you bit her in the arm."

Me neither. I was aiming for her face.

I poured myself a wee tankard of Chardonnay to recuperate and was reaching for a restorative dose of Oreos when the phone rang.

Too wiped out to answer, I let the machine get it.

"Jaine, it's Patti Marshall."

I froze in my tracks. Patti had been the queen bee of my alma mater, Hermosa High, a social despot who ruled her subjects with a fine-tuned cruelty and a flawless complexion.

Her voice drifted from the machine, the same nasal whine that had delivered so many devastating zingers in the girls' locker room.

"I heard you're a writer now. Give me a call, okay? I think I may have some work for you."

My palms turned clammy. Patti represented everything I'd loathed about high school. I could just picture her sitting at her throne at the Popular Table in the cafeteria, eyeing the Unpopulars with undisguised disdain and leading her Bitches in Waiting in a chorus of derisive giggles.

I would've liked nothing more than to zap her message to oblivion. But she'd said the magic word—work—a commodity I'm chronically short of.

I turned to Prozac who was sprawled out on the sofa, licking her prized privates.

"What do you think, Pro? She's a world-class rat, but I really need the money. What should I do?"

She looked up at me with big green eyes that seemed to say, *It's always about you, isn't it? What about me? When do I eat?*

Which goes a long toward explaining why man's best friend has never been the cat.

Oh, well. I really needed the dough, so I took a bracing gulp of Chardonnay and forced myself to give Patti a call.

"Hi, Jaine!" she trilled when she came on the line. "How've you been?"

Somewhat stunned by the friendly lilt to her voice, I mumbled, "Um. Fine."

"Listen, I've got great news. I'm getting married."

"Congratulations."

I didn't envy the poor guy headed down that aisle.

"Anyhow, I need somebody to write my wedding vows. I heard you're a writer now, and I thought it'd be great to work with an old friend."

An old friend? The woman was clearly smoking something illegal.

"So what have you written? Anything I've heard of?"

As a matter of fact, I had written an ad she might very well have heard of. Or at least seen; it's been on bus stops all over town. But it wasn't exactly the kind of ad that leaves people awestruck.

"I wrote *In a Rush to Flush? Call Toiletmasters.*"

I waited for Patti's patented, *Ewww, gross!*, the line with which she tarred many a fragile ego at Hermosa High, but instead, I heard:

"Really? I saw that in the Yellow Pages. It's very cute!"

Alert the media. A compliment. From Catty Patti.

"So how about it, Jaine? You think you'd be interested?"

"Well—"

"I was thinking of paying somewhere in the neighborhood of three thousand dollars."

Call the movers. That was my kind of neighborhood.

"That sounds terrific, Patti. I'd love to do it."

"Wonderful!" she gushed. "I know we're going to have so much fun!"

We agreed to meet the next day and I hung up, not quite believing what had just happened.

This certainly wasn't the same Queen of Mean I'd known in high school. Was it possible Patti had changed over the years? Why not? People changed all the time. I had to stop being such a cynic and give her the benefit of the doubt.

Somewhere along the line Patti Marshall had obviously morphed into a decent human being. And more important, a decent human being who was willing to enrich my bank balance by three grand.

And so I embarked on my new assignment filled with hope and good cheer—much like I imagine Dr. Graham must have felt before reaching for Prozac's privates.

Chapter 2

I arranged to meet Patti the next day at her parents' home in Bel Air.

Back in Hermosa, Patti had lived in a fabulous beachfront house, a gleaming white affair with unobstructed views of the Pacific. A house, needless to say, I'd never been invited to.

As nice as Patti's Hermosa house had been, it was a virtual shack compared to her new digs in Bel Air. As I drove up the leafy pathway to the estate—a sprawling manse with more wings than a condo complex—I could practically smell the scent of freshly minted money in the air.

I parked my ancient Corolla in the "motor court" and checked my reflection in the rearview mirror. It was glorious day, sunny and clear, and I was grateful that my hair—which usually turns to Brillo at the first sign of humidity—was mercifully frizz-free. I fluffed it into what I hoped was a Sarah Jessica Parker-ish nimbus of curls, then sucked in my gut and headed for the front door.

A Hispanic maid in a starched white apron answered the bell.

"I'm here to see Patti," I said. "I'm Jaine Austen, her writer."

"Another one?"

She rolled her eyes and ushered me into a foyer bigger than

my living room, complete with double marble staircase and a crystal chandelier the size of a Volkswagen.

"Ms. Patti," she called up the steps, "the writer lady is here."

Patti's voice drifted from above. "I'll be right down."

"Good luck." The maid shot me a sympathetic smile and scurried away.

I was standing there, counting the crystals in the chandelier, when I heard the clack of heels on the marble stairs.

I looked up and there she was, Patti Marshall, Hermosa High's very own Cruella De Vil. I'd been hoping she'd put on a few pounds since high school like the rest of us mere mortals. But if anything, she'd lost weight. Life sure isn't fair, isn't it?

Unlike most high school prima donnas, Patti had never been a conventional beauty. Her face was a little too long, her eyes just a little too close together. But there was something about the way she carried herself, the way she looked at you through those close-set eyes, that had you convinced she was a stunner.

She made her grand entrance now, sweeping down the stairs in body-hugging capris and tank top. Her gleaming blond hair, always her best feature, was caught up in a careless ponytail that swished from side to side as she walked.

In the crook of her arm, she carried what at first looked like a large cotton ball, but when the cotton ball started yapping, I realized it was a dog.

"Jaine, sweetie!" she beamed. "It's so good to see you again."

As she wrapped me in a bony one-armed hug, her dog began licking my face with all the abandon of a coed gone wild.

"Mamie really likes you, Jaine!"

Either that, or she smelled the Quarter Pounder I'd had for lunch.

"It's time you two were properly introduced."

She held out the dog, and I now saw that they were wearing matching pink tank tops, embroidered with the logo *I'm Cute. Buy Me Something.*

"Jaine, say hello to Mamie." She smiled at me expectantly.

Oh, good heavens. She actually wanted me to say hello to her dog.

"Um, hello, Mamie." I managed a feeble smile.

Mamie, having clearly decided I was her new best friend, squirmed in Patti's arms, eager to unleash her salivary glands on me.

"I hardly ever let anybody do this," Patti intoned with all the solemnity of King Arthur bestowing a knighthood, "but you can hold her."

With that, she thrust the dog in my arms, and within seconds I was covered in an aromatic layer of dog spit.

"Let's go out to the patio, and I'll tell you all about your assignment."

She guided me past a maze of impeccably decorated rooms and then out through French doors to a bit of paradise that would give the Garden of Eden a run for its money.

I gazed in awe at the plushly furnished patio (complete with built-in Viking BBQ), the olympic-caliber lap pool, and the tennis courts in the distance—all of it surrounded by velvety green lawns, exquisitely tended flower beds, and a small forest of trees.

"Want something to eat?" Patti asked, plopping down onto a chaise longue. "I'm starved."

"Sure," I said, hoping for something whose main ingredient was chocolate.

"Hey, Rosa," she barked into an intercom on an end table. "Bring us some Evian and carrot sticks."

Oh, foo. Not exactly the snack I'd been hoping for.

"So what happened to your house in Hermosa Beach?" I asked, easing myself into a pillowy armchair, still holding Mamie, who was now busy nibbling on my ears.

"Oh, Mom sold it when she married Connie."

"Connie?"

I blinked in surprise. I remembered Patti's mom, a va-va-va voom blonde with a nipped-in waist and man-made bosoms, and somehow I couldn't picture her hooked up with someone of the female persuasion.

"Short for Conrad. Conrad Devane. My stepfather."

"Where's your dad?"

"Oh, Daddy died about ten years ago. Guess he figured it was easier than living with Mom. He wasn't dead in his grave two weeks before Mom sank her claws into Connie. She knows how to sniff out the rich ones. Not that it mattered to me. Daddy left me a bundle."

She smiled proudly as if inheriting money was a major life accomplishment.

"Anyhow, we decided to have the wedding here at the house. It's so much cozier than a hotel, don't you think?"

Was she kidding? This place *was* a hotel.

"We'll have the ceremony out on the lawn. It should be utterly glorious."

She stretched out on the chaise, then shrieked, "Hey, Rosa! Where the hell's our food?—Oh, there you are. It's about time."

I looked up to see the harried maid scurrying to our side, with two frosty bottles of Evian and carrot sticks, beautifully arranged in a cut glass bowl.

Patti grabbed an Evian from the tray and pouted.

"Yuck, Rosa. This water's too cold. How many times do I have to tell you, I want it chilled, not icy?"

"Shall I bring you another, Ms. Patti?" Rosa asked through gritted teeth.

"Oh, forget it," Patti said, with an irritated wave. "Just go."

More than happy to escape, Rosa scooted back into the house.

As I watched her retreating figure, it occurred to me that perhaps I'd been a tad optimistic thinking that Patti had miraculously morphed into a sweetheart since high school.

"Like I said on the phone," she said, reaching for a carrot stick, "I need somebody to help me write my wedding vows. You wouldn't believe how many writers I've been through."

After the little scene I'd just witnessesed, I had no trouble believing it. None whatsoever.

"I'm counting on you, Jaine, to come through for me."

The look in her eyes told me it wasn't so much a wish as a royal edict.

"What sort of vows were you thinking of?"

"I've had the most fabulous idea." Her eyes lit up. "Instead of a traditional ceremony, I've decided to reenact the balcony scene from *Romeo and Juliet*."

Huh?

"Only this time, with a happy ending!"

For a minute I wondered if Mamie's spit in my ear had affected my hearing.

"I'll be up on that balcony." She pointed to an elaborate wrought iron balcony on the second story of the house. "My fiancé will stand below and when I ask him to 'deny thy father and refuse thy name,' he's going to say 'okey doke,' and then instead of all that gloomy-doomy suicide stuff, I'll come down and marry him. See? A happy ending!"

By now, even Mamie's jaw was hanging open with disbelief.

And for the first time it hit me that Patti Marshall was an idiot. All those years at Hermosa High, we were terrorized by a prized num-num.

"It's really a very simple assignment, Jaine. All you have to do is—"

"Rewrite William Shakespeare."

"Yes! Make it hip and modern! Isn't that the best idea ever?"

Compared to what? The Spanish Inquisition?

"C'mon," she said, jumping up from the chaise, "let's go up to the balcony. Once you see how gorgeous it is, it'll put you in the mood to write."

The only thing that would put me in the mood to write this bilge would be a lobotomy.

With Mamie still in my arms, I followed Patti back inside the house and up to her bedroom, a hot pink extravaganza (think Fleer's Dubble Bubble) that led out onto the balcony.

"Inspirational, isn't it?" Patti gushed as we stepped outside.

"Um. Very."

"How do you like the railing?"

I dutifully oohed and aahed over the elaborate wrought iron scrollwork that bordered the balcony.

"I had it imported all the way from Verona, Italy," she beamed. "That's where the real Romeo and Juliet were born."

I didn't want to bust her bubble and tell her that Romeo and Juliet were fictional characters, so just I kept oohing and aahing.

"The workmen just finished installing it yesterday. And I've ordered statues of Cupid that'll be scattered around the garden. Won't that be romantic?"

Somehow I managed to nod yes.

At which point, she draped herself over the railing and, with great gusto, began mangling Shakespeare:

"Romeo, Romeo, wherefort ares't thou, Romeo?"

At the sound of this exceedingly bad line reading, Mamie let out a plaintive yowl, as did Shakespeare, no doubt, from his grave.

I joined Patti at the railing and gazed down at the rolling green landscape below.

"That's where Dickie proposed to me," she said, pointing to a wooden gazebo nestled in a bower of trees. "The Secret Gazebo."

"The Secret Gazebo?"

"We call it that because you can only see it from up here on the balcony. It's practically impossible to find down on the ground unless you know where it is."

"A secret gazebo. How romantic."

"I'll say. I've had some pretty kinky sex down there."

Luckily, she spared me the details.

After assuring Patti that I'd been sufficiently "inspired," we trooped back downstairs where she took Mamie from my drool-infested arms.

"So now you know the assignment," she said with a toss of her ponytail. "Just dash off a scene where Romeo proposes to me, and I say yes. Only of course, Juliet's name will be Patti, and Romeo's name will be Dickie. And get rid of all the stuffy language. I want it to be snappy and sassy. Like *Friends* with swords and long dresses."

By now I was on Auto Nod, bobbing my head at everything she said, no matter how inane. Five more minutes with her, and I'd need a neck brace.

"C'mon," she said, "I'll walk you to your car."

We headed outside just in time to see a bright yellow VW beetle pull up in the driveway.

"Oh, look, it's Dickie!"

A tall, sandy-haired guy untangled his long legs from the car.

"Dickie, sweetie!" Patti cried, racing to his side.

She threw her arms around his neck and locked her lips on his. When they finally came up for air, she said, "Honey, say hello to Jaine. I told you I hired her to write our wedding vows, didn't I?—You remember Dickie, don't you, Jaine?"

I looked up at her fiancé and took in his shy smile and spiky, slightly tousled hair. There was something about that smile of his that seemed familiar, but I couldn't quite place him.

"I'm afraid not."

"It's Dickie Potter. He was in our class at Hermosa."

"Dickie Potter?" I blinked in surprise. "The same Dickie Potter who played tuba in the marching band?"

He nodded.

When I last saw Dickie Potter, he was a committed nerd, all knees and elbows, his face sprinkled with acne, someone Patti never would have looked at twice. But over the years, he'd blossomed into a major cutie.

"What a change, huh?" Patti winked.

"Patti and I ran into each other at last year's Hermosa High reunion," Dickie said, gazing at her with a worshipful smile.

"Yeah, he took one look at me, and the next thing I knew he was divorcing his wife."

Patti giggled coyly, the happy homewrecker.

"Poor Normalynne," she said, without a trace of sympathy. "Didn't know what hit her."

"Normalynne Butler?" I asked, remembering a tall, gawky girl who played flute in the band. "You were married to Normalynne?"

"Yes." Dickie nodded ruefully. "I'm really sorry it ended the way it did."

"Oh, poo. I'm sure she's over it by now," Patti said, waving away his doubts. "Well, it's time for Jaine to get out of here and leave us alone."

She threw her arms around him once more, clearly ready for some wild times in the gazebo.

"It was nice seeing you," Dickie said to me, over her shoulder.

"Very nice," I said, eager to make my escape before the action got X-rated. I gave a feeble wave and was heading for my car, when Patti called out to me.

"You better not screw this up, Jaine, like you used to screw up in P.E." She shot me the same demoralizing look she'd used so effectively all those years ago in the Hermosa High gym. "You were such a klutz."

Then she laughed a tinkly laugh for Dickie's benefit. She wanted him to think she was kidding. But she and I both knew better.

"And don't take too long," she trilled. "I want the script in my hands the day after tomorrow."

So much for Patti having changed. Whatever initial burst of goodwill she'd shown me was history.

The bitch was back.

I trudged up the path to my apartment, wondering how I was going to survive working for Patti, when I saw my neighbor Lance stretched out on a deck chair.

Lance and I live in a modest duplex on the fringes of Beverly Hills, far from the megamansions to the north and just a hop, skip, and jump away from the gangs to the south. It's a neat old 1940s building where the rent is reasonable and the plumbing impossible.

"Hey, Jaine," Lance said, his blond curls glinting in the sun. "How's it going?"

"Don't ask," I grunted.

"C'mere," he said, patting his chair. "Tell Uncle Lance all about it."

Lance works odd hours as a shoe salesman at Neiman Marcus, which is why he can often be found lolling about on deck chairs in the middle of the day.

I plopped down next to him and he put a comforting arm around my shoulder. An arm he promptly jerked away.

"Yuck. Why are you wet? And you smell funny."

"It's dog spit. One of the perks of my new job," I sighed. "I just got the assignment from hell, writing for a ghastly woman I used to go to high school with. A world-class bitch, the queen of mean."

"Any chance she's gained oodles of weight and grown a mustache since high school?"

I shook my head, dispirited. "Patti's actually thinner than she was back then."

"That's because the mean gene burns calories. That's your problem, Jaine," he said, glancing at my thighs. "You're way too nice."

"She actually wants me to rewrite Shakespeare. She wants me to make it 'snappy.' Like *Friends* with swords and long dresses."

"Why don't you just turn down the job?"

"Oh, I don't know. I was hoping to spend the money on a few luxuries like food and rent."

"Poor baby," he tsked. "Know what you need? A nice frosty margarita. C'mon, let's go to my apartment and I'll make you one. With a big bowl of chips."

"Great," I said, my taste buds springing to life.

"Oh, wait. I just remembered. I'm all out of tequila. And margarita mix. And chips, too, for that matter."

Five minutes later we were sitting in my living room feasting on lukewarm Snapples and leftover martini olives.

"It's funny," I said, sucking on a pimento. "You spend decades trying to forget how miserable you were in high school, and then, after only a few minutes with the Class Dragon Lady, it all comes flooding back." I took a desultory slurp of Snapple. "I was so awkward in high school. I swear, I spent four years with the same damn zit on my chin. What about you? Were you a mess?"

"Not really," Lance said with an apologetic shrug. "I had my own set of problems, trying to explain to my dad why I wasn't reading *Playboy* and playing football, but I didn't go through an awkward phase."

Prozac looked up from where she was nestled on Lance's lap.

Me, neither. I've always been adorable.

"You can't let this Patti creature make you feel bad about yourself," Lance said, with an indignant shake of his curls. "You've got to do something to boost your self-confidence." His brow furrowed in thought. "You know what you need?"

"Yes," I said. "A frosty margarita. But if memory serves, you're all out of tequila."

"You need a new look! An entire wardrobe makeover!"

His eyes shone with evangelical fervor. Lance has been dying to do a Henry Higgins on me for years.

"Forget it, Lance. I can't afford to go shopping."

"Okay, then, we'll do the next best thing—closet therapy. With me as your closet therapist."

"My closet therapist?"

"Yes. I'll get rid of all the ghastly clothes in your closet you shouldn't be caught dead in and then put together some adorable outfits, so you can show Patti what a hot number you really are."

"Really, Lance. I don't care what Patti thinks of me."

"Of course, you do. Now c'mon. It's time for closet therapy!"

And with that he took me by the arm and marched me to my bedroom closet.

"Gaaack!" he cried, surveying its contents. "It's worse than I remembered."

For some odd reason, Lance is convinced I have terrible taste in clothes. According to him, moths come to my closet to commit suicide.

"Anyhow, here's how closet therapy works," he said, getting down to business. "You make three piles. The clothes you're going to keep. The clothes you're going to give to charity. And the clothes so hideous even Goodwill won't take them. Are you ready to start?"

I nodded with a distinct lack of enthusiasm.

"Here we go."

He grabbed a perfectly lovely striped blouse and held it up.

"Gaack! Polyester!" he shuddered, tossing it onto floor. "Into the Hideous Pile. Omigod. And look at this jacket. Where did you buy it? A Russian thrift shop? And a *Cuckoo for Cocoa Puffs* T-shirt! I may go blind!"

It shows you how much he knew. That T-shirt happened to be a collector's item.

I plopped down on my bed and watched as he tossed one perfectly usable item of clothing after another onto the Hideous Pile until my closet was a graveyard of wire hangers.

"Are you sure you can't afford to go shopping?" Lance said, surveying the wreckage.

"No, Lance, I can't."

"Well, then, Houston, I think we've got a problem."

He was staring at a lone cocktail dress that had survived the massacre, when his cell phone rang. He checked his caller ID, then grabbed it eagerly.

"Hi, Kevin! Great to hear from you. . . . When? . . . Now? Sure, I'm not doing anything. I'll be right over!"

He hung up and turned to me, smiling sheepishly.

"Don't kill me, Jaine, but I've gotta go. I'm meeting Kevin at the movies. Did I tell you about Kevin? No? Well, I think he could be Mr. Right. We met the other night on line at the yogurt parlor. He's a nonfat cherry vanilla, just like me.

"Don't worry," he said, waving to the mountain of clothing in the Hideous Pile. "I'll help you clean up this mess later tonight. Well, maybe not tonight. But tomorrow for sure. Or the day after."

And with that he blew out the door so fast, he practically left exhaust fumes.

I got up with a sigh and plucked Prozac from where she was napping on the Hideous Pile.

Then, one by one, I began hanging my fashion rejects back in my closet.

When I was all done, I caught my reflection in the mirror on the back of the closet door. There on my chin was the start of a blockbuster zit.

Yep, it was beginning to feel a lot like high school.

Chapter 3

It wasn't easy turning *Romeo and Juliet* into an episode of *Friends*, but with a positive attitude and a fistful of Excedrin, somehow I managed it.

Two days later I had the finished pages in my hot little hands and set out to deliver them to Patti. We'd arranged to meet at the bridal salon where she and her bridesmaids were being fitted for their gowns.

"You'll never guess who my bridesmaids are," she'd said on the phone when we'd set up the date. "Cheryl and Denise!"

Oh, yuck. Cheryl Hogan and Denise Gilbert were Patti's two best friends from high school—Denise, a striking brunette; and Cheryl, a delicate blonde with enormous Betty Boop eyes. Together with Patti, they formed a most unholy alliance—the Terrible Trinity, I used to call them.

They had this way of collectively scanning you, zeroing in on your latest zit or bad hair day with the unerring accuracy of an MRI.

"Won't it be fun," Patti had gushed, "the four of us getting together again?"

Yeah, right. About as much fun as gastric bypass surgery.

I made my way over to Cynthia's Bridal Salon in the tony Montana Avenue section of Santa Monica, where the valet parking cost more than my car. I circled the block a few zillion times searching for a space on the street, but there hasn't been an open parking space on Montana since D.W. Griffith was shooting *Birth of a Nation*, so eventually I had to admit defeat and toss my keys to the valet.

He drove off with a frightening squeal, and I walked the few steps to Cynthia's, my palms gushing sweat. I told myself I was being ridiculous. I couldn't let the Terrible Trinity intimidate me anymore. It had been almost twenty years since graduation. I was an award-winning writer with an impressive career writing toilet bowl ads.

Okay, so maybe writing toilet bowl ads wasn't so impressive. And maybe the only award I'd ever won was the Golden Plunger award from the Los Angeles Plumbers Association. But it paid the rent, didn't it? Well, not always. Sometimes I had to get cash advances on my credit card. Which reminded me, if I didn't pay my MasterCard bill soon, I'd be hit with another late fee. And ditto for my Nordstrom bill. And Bloomingdale's. Not to mention the bills from the phone company and my dentist. By now I was in a funk just thinking of all the money I owed.

All I can say is it's a good thing I don't make my living giving pep talks.

With a weary sigh, I pushed open Cynthia's country French doors and headed inside.

Cynthia's was a plush cocoon of ankle-deep carpeting and flattering lighting. Soothing classical music tinkled in the lavender-scented air. I looked around and was relieved to see that Patti was the only customer in the store. Maybe there'd been a change of plans and Cheryl and Denise weren't going to be there after all.

Patti stood on a raised platform in her wedding gown, a froufrou Renaissance-inspired number with a low-cut bodice, puffy sleeves, and enough material in the train to upholster a hotel lobby.

A seamstress knelt at her feet, pins in her mouth, making alterations, while an elegant older woman, her silver hair swept back in a chignon, stood by with a nervous smile on her face.

"Cynthia, how many times do I have to tell you?" Patti snapped. "I want the bodice lower."

Was she insane? If that dress were cut any lower, it would be a belt.

"Are you sure?" the silver-haired woman asked, a noticeable tic in her left eye.

"Yes, I'm sure. I paid good money for these boobs. I want everyone to see them."

She then turned and saw me. "Oh, hi, Jaine. You have the script?"

"Right here," I said, waving the pages. "I think it turned out very well."

"I'll be the judge of that."

And at that moment I knew without a doubt that I'd be rewriting this script right up until she and Dickie said "I do," sweating bullets for every one of those three thousand dollars.

I was standing there, wondering if it was worth it, when a stunning brunette stepped out of one of the dressing rooms. With a sinking sensation, I realized it was Denise Gilbert.

The dewy good looks of her youth had been replaced by an air of sleek sophistication. But basically she was the same beauty she'd always been—only thinner. Was there no justice in the world? Was I the only Hermosa High grad who'd packed on a pound or two?

"What do you think, Patti?" she asked, twirling around in her dress.

It's not easy to look chic in a bridesmaid's dress with big puffy sleeves and a bow in back, but somehow Denise managed to pull it off.

Patti's eyes narrowed.

"The bow needs to be bigger."

"But Ms. Marshall," Cynthia protested, "if we make it any bigger, it's not going to be very flattering."

Of course it wouldn't. That's why Patti asked for it. You didn't have to be Siggy Freud to figure out that the last thing Patti wanted was to be upstaged by a stunning bridesmaid.

"Besides," Cynthia said, her tic more noticeable than ever, "I'm not sure we'll have time to import more fabric in time for the wedding."

Patti shot her a look that could melt steel.

"Make time."

"Yes, of course. Of course." By now poor Cynthia's tic was out of control. "I'll go see to it now."

She and the seamstress scurried off into the back room, no doubt to hit the vodka bottle.

Throughout the preceding exchange Denise had just stood there, smiling pleasantly, her face an impassive mask.

"Jaine," she said now, noticing me for the first time. "Patti told me you'd be here. How nice to see you."

Her eyes raked me over.

"You haven't changed a bit."

Translation: *My God. She still has that same zit on her chin.*

"You, either," I said. "So how've you been?"

"Wonderful," she said. "I'm an attorney now."

Thin *and* rich. How depressing.

"And what about you, Jaine? What have you been up to?"

"As Patti probably told you, I'm a writer."

"Yes, she did mention it. *In a Rush to Flush? Call Toiletmasters.* How clever."

Was there just the tiniest trace of a snicker in her smile?

"And what else is going on in your life?"

"Yes, Jaine," Patti chimed in. "I meant to ask you. Any men in your life? You married?"

"No, not married."

I didn't tell them about my ex-husband, The Blob, a guy who wore flip-flops to our wedding and watched ESPN during sex. Somehow I didn't think they'd be impressed.

"Any boyfriends?" Denise asked.

"Yeah," Patti echoed. "Any boyfriends?"

They shot me laser beam looks. And suddenly I was back in the hallway at Hermosa High, wilting under their supercilious gazes, a newborn zit ablaze on my chin.

"So, Jaine? What about it?" Patti wasn't about to let me off the hook. "Any special guy in your life?"

"As a matter fact, yes."

Where had that come from? The only special guy in my life was the Domino's delivery guy.

"I'm engaged to be married."

Huh?

"To a doctor."

What the hell was I saying?

"Yes." I persisted in my madness. "A neurosurgeon."

Maybe it was some form of Tourette's.

"Right," said Patti. She and Denise exchanged sidelong glances, skepticism oozing from their pores. They weren't buying any of this. Not for a second.

"Congratulations," Denise said dryly.

"I just had the most wonderful idea!" Patti cooed, a nasty glint in her eye. "You and your neurosurgeon fiancé simply must come to my wedding."

Okay, no need to panic. I'd just tell her my fiancé was out of town. Yes, he was in Africa, helping sick Africans. I'd tell her I was flying there to join him. And we couldn't possibly make it to her wedding.

The words that actually came out of my mouth, however, went something like this:

"Francois and I would be delighted to come to your wedding."

Francois??? Had I totally lost my mind??

I was about to commit myself to the home for the terminally mendacious when a pudgy woman in a polyester jogging suit walked in the shop. She glanced around timidly, then waved when she spotted Patti and Denise.

Patti took one look at her and went ballistic.

"Cheryl!" she hissed. "You look awful."

Cheryl? Was this frumpy woman with the frizzed-out hair the same delicate beauty I'd known in high school? At last I'd run into someone who'd packed on some pounds since graduation. But for some reason, it didn't feel nearly as gratifying as I thought it would.

"For crying out loud, Cheryl," Patti snapped. "You promised you'd lose weight."

Cheryl stood there, red-faced with shame.

"I'm sorry, Patti. I tried. Really I did."

"Did you eat all the Jenny Craig meals I sent?"

"Yes," she murmured, eyes lowered, like a kid called to the principal's office.

"Probably all in one day," Patti sneered. "You realize the wedding's next week?"

Cheryl nodded.

"You'll never lose the weight by then. And I can't possibly have a fat bridesmaid. You know what that means, don't you?"

Cheryl nodded again.

"You're out!" Patti said, with all the finesse of a guillotine beheading. "You're no longer in the wedding party."

"I'm so sorry, Patti," Cheryl mumbled, eyes still lowered.

"You should be. Do you realize how difficult you're making things for me? Where the hell am I going to get another bridesmaid at this late date?"

She gazed in my direction for the briefest instant, but then looked away, having clearly dismissed me as unsuitable wedding party material.

"Oh, well," she sighed, the bridal martyr, "I'll manage somehow. I always do."

At last Cheryl looked up, and I saw that her big blue eyes, always her best feature, were blinking back tears.

In spite of how mean she'd been in high school, I felt sorry for her. And actually, when I thought about it, Cheryl hadn't really been all that mean. It was always Patti who'd been the nasty one, the instigator. Cheryl and Denise had been more of a Greek chorus, backing her up in her many acts of torture.

I had a fleeting impulse to put my arm around Cheryl and console her with the dusty Almond Joy in the bottom of my purse.

But I didn't, of course. I had troubles enough of my own. In case you forgot, I had less than a week to find myself a fiancé. A neurosurgeon, yet. Named Francois.

"A neurosurgeon fiancé? Have you lost your mind?"

I was sitting across from my best friend, Kandi Tobolowski, at our favorite restaurant, Paco's Tacos, a colorful joint with burritos the size of cruise missiles.

"How could you tell such a whopper?" Kandi stared at me, wide-eyed. "Couldn't you have made him something more believable, like a dermatologist?"

"You're missing the point here, Kandi. It doesn't matter what sort of doctor he is. What matters is, he doesn't exist."

I stared morosely at my Chimichanga Combo Plate. Why the heck had I ordered such a calorie-fest? I should be eating something sensible like Kandi's mahimahi if I wanted to look decent for the wedding.

"I still can't understand why you did it," she said, taking a dainty bite of her fish.

"I don't know." I sighed. "It was just like the time in high school when Patti and Denise cornered me in the locker room and asked me if I had a date for the prom. They knew I didn't, but they wanted to see me squirm. So I lied and said I had one."

"How'd you weasel your way out of that?"

"Well," I said, thinking back to those long-gone days, "there was this guy at school I was interested in. His name was Dylan. He'd just transferred from back east. He had huge brown eyes and a sad soulful look. Everywhere he went he carried a copy of Nietzsche's *Thus Spake Zarathustra*. For some reason, that impressed the heck out of me. I couldn't believe that there among the beach bunny heathens at Hermosa High was an actual eastern intellectual.

"So I decided to ask him to the prom. I figured what the heck. I had nothing to lose. I spent hours in front of the mirror, rehearsing what I was going to say. Finally I got up my courage to approach him. He was sitting in the schoolyard, staring out into the horizon, his copy of Nietzsche on his lap. Somehow I managed to sputter an invitation."

"And? What did he say?"

By now Kandi's mahimahi was forgotten on her plate. Kandi often forgets to eat, one of the reasons why she, unlike yours truly, can step on the scale at the doctor's office without breaking into a cold sweat.

"He said yes."

"Wow," Kandi grinned. "So lying paid off."

"Not exactly," I sighed. "Don't forget, I'd never actually had a conversation with the guy. He showed up at my house the night of the prom reeking of marijuana. That Nietzsche book of his wasn't a book at all, but a hollowed-out box where he kept his drug supplies. The guy had a vocabulary of about six words and five of them were, 'Hey baby, wanna get high?'"

"Omigod, this is as bad as my prom. I went with my cousin Barry. I could've killed him. He spent the whole night at the punch bowl flirting with Mrs. Handler, my English teacher. When I think of all the hours I spent shopping for my prom dress—"

"Kandi, could we please stick to my nightmare?"

"Right," she said. "Sorry. So what did you do?"

"What could I do? I had to show up at the prom to prove to Patti and Denise that I had a date."

"Did they see you?"

"They saw me, all right. In addition to being a pothead, Dylan was an awful dancer. And not just run-of-the-mill awful. Extravagantly awful. He spun and dipped and swirled me so much, I felt like a human salad spinner.

"At a certain point, everybody cleared off the dance floor to watch us. I could see Patti and her gang standing on the sidelines, enjoying every second of my misery.

"At last the song came to an end. And that's when Dylan gave me one final spin. Only this time, he let go of my hand. And the next thing I knew I was spinning across the floor and straight into Principal Seawright's lap."

"Omigod," Kandi gasped. "You landed in the principal's lap? What did he say?"

"If memory serves, his exact words were: *I believe this seat is already taken*."

"Oh, wow."

"If I live to be a thousand, I'll never forget the expression on his face. I practically got frostbite just looking at him. Honest, Kandi, I thought I was going to die."

Having finished my tale of woe, I picked up my fork to dig into my dinner and saw to my amazement that I'd somehow managed to polish off every bite of my Chimichanga Combo Plate. Can somebody please explain how I'd done all the talking and yet Kandi was the one whose dinner was practically untouched?

Well, that was it, I vowed. Not another bite of food would pass my lips. I simply could not afford to gain a single ounce for the wedding.

"Ah," Kandi said, shaking her head solemnly, "what a tangled web we weave when we practice to deceive."

"What??" I gasped.

"I'm sorry, Jaine, but that's what you get for lying."

"My God, Kandi. Look who's talking. The woman who pretended to be an alcoholic so she could meet guys at AA."

"Oh, please. That's entirely different."

"And just how is it different?"

"Don't you remember? I met that cute stockbroker. We dated for three months before he fell off the wagon and ran off with a barmaid. *My* story had a happy ending. For a while at least."

The woman's logic defies explanation.

"So what are you going to do about your date for the wedding?" she asked, pushing her refried beans to the side of her plate out of eating range.

"I have absolutely no idea."

"You want me to fix you up with one of the insects on my show?"

The insects to whom Kandi referred were the actors on *Beanie & the Cockroach*, the animated cartoon show where Kandi toils as a writer.

"I think Manny the Mole might be available. He's a really nice guy, if you don't mind your neurosurgeon being 5'3" in his elevator shoes."

"Let's save Manny for plan B."

"I know! How about an escort service?"

"An escort service? Are you crazy??"

"They're listed in the Yellow Pages."

Well, dear reader, if you think I was about to degrade myself by paying for a date with a guy who was just one step up from a male hooker, all I can say is—you're a very perceptive reader.

"I'll call first thing tomorrow," I said, reaching for a forkful of Kandi's refried beans.

YOU'VE GOT MAIL

To: Jausten
From: Shoptillyoudrop
Subject: Marvelous News!

Jaine, honey, you'll never guess who's coming to stay with us. Roberto Scaffaro! I told you about Roberto, didn't I, the darling young man I met in Rome the summer I graduated from high school? He was a waiter at the pensione where I was staying. Every day after work he showed me around the city to charming places I never would have discovered in the guidebooks.

He didn't speak a word of English and I didn't speak any Italian but we used my Italian–English dictionary and had the time of our lives. I'll never forget the night we ate al fresco on the Spanish Steps. Or is it al dente? I always get those two confused. All I know is that it was a picnic, and it was magnifico!

And to think that was all more than forty years ago! Over the years we've exchanged Christmas cards, and then just the other day I got a letter from one of his children (Roberto's English is still pretty terrible) telling me that Roberto's wife died last year and that he's coming to the states to visit his son who lives in Arizona. And he wants to stop off first to see me.

I wrote back and told him come right over "presto." That's Italian for "quickly." Or is it "prego"? Or is that a spaghetti sauce? Oh, dear. I guess my Italian's still pretty terrible, too. Anyhow, I insisted he stay here at the condo, and I can't wait to see him.

Of course, the place is a disgrace. I absolutely must change the curtains in the guest bedroom and get some new towels. I saw some fabulous Egyptian towels on the shopping channel, a whole set for just $29.95, plus shipping and handling. If I put in my order now, they'll be here in time for Roberto's visit. I can't possibly have him using the ratty old guest towels we've had since you were in kindergarten.

Must run, darling, and place my order before they sell out.

Arrivederci!

Mom

To: Jausten
From: DaddyO
Subject: Steams My Beans

Hi, Lambchop—

Have you heard the news? Your mother's former lover is coming to stay with us. I consider myself a pretty open-minded fellow, but the thought of having her old "amore" stay under my own roof just steams my beans.

Your mom insists nothing went on between them, but I wasn't born yesterday. I know those Italian guys and their animal magnetism.

Oh, well. It's a good thing I'm not the jealous type— Whoops. Gotta go, sweetpea. The mailman's here and I need to screen the mail for love letters from Italy.

Love & kisses from,

Daddy

To: Jausten
From: Shoptillyoudrop
Subject: Did You Ever Hear Anything So Silly?

Daddy's impossible. He's convinced Roberto and I were lovers! For heaven's sake, Jaine, I met Roberto when I was eighteen years old, back in the years when young women waited to get married before they had "ex-say," if you get my drift.

Honestly, Jaine, I think Roberto kissed me once the night before I left to come back home, but it was all so innocent. Now your father is running around acting like we left a trail of blazing mattresses across Italy. Of course, it doesn't help that Roberto's wife died last year. Daddy's convinced he's coming here to make me his new signora.

Did you ever hear of anything so silly? I'll bet by now Roberto's a fat middle-aged man with a potbelly and no hair.

XOXO,

Mom

To: Jausten
From: DaddyO
Subject: Rigatoni Romeo

Just what I was afraid of. Another letter from your mom's boyfriend. This time he sent his picture. Typical continental casanova. Tall, dark, and what some people might call handsome. You should've seen your mother swoon. You can't tell me they weren't a hot ticket back in Italy. If she thinks I'm helping her hang new curtains for that rigatoni romeo, she's sadly mistaken.

I'm off to the library to return a book. And I just may stop off for a hot fudge sundae on my way home. I'm supposed to be watching my cholesterol, but who cares if I clog my arteries? Certainly not your mother. She's too busy fixing up the guest bedroom for her future husband.

Lots of love from your poor neglected,

Daddy

Chapter 4

I suppose I should be grateful that my parents are leading active lives in their retirement years. And I am. But I'd be a lot more grateful if they weren't such crazymakers.

When I say "they" I refer, of course, to Daddy. He's the prime crazymaker in our family, with Mom a pale sidekick in their white knuckle escapades.

Mom is not without her own quirks, however. She was the one who insisted on moving three thousand miles away from a perfectly lovely house in Hermosa Beach—all the way to Tampa Vistas, Florida—so she could be close to the Home Shopping Channel. I tried to explain that she wouldn't get her packages any faster that way, but my explanations fell on deaf ears. Besides, she said, it would be "fun" living in such close proximity to her favorite shopping channel hosts.

But it's Daddy who holds the World Champion Crazymaker title. He has single-handedly driven more people to distraction than telemarketing, control top panty hose, and Hare Krishnas combined. I had no doubt that Mom's relationship with Roberto had been as innocent as a Hallmark special. But I knew it was just a matter of time before Daddy turned this molehill into a Himalayan-sized headache. Sooner or later, somebody's blood pressure would go soaring. (And by "somebody," of course, I meant me.)

But that morning my parents were small potatoes in my

supermarket cart of woes, overshadowed by my desperate need to come up with a "fiancé" for Patti's wedding.

Which is why, right after breakfast, I started thumbing through the Yellow Pages under "Escort Services."

I would've had an easy time of it if I'd been in the market for "a beautiful girl at my door guaranteed." When it came to escorts, the Yellow Pages was definitely not an equal opportunity supplier. All they had to offer were hot times with pouty-lipped nymphettes named Desiree and Angelique.

So I toddled over to my computer and tried my luck with Google. Unfortunately, when I typed in "Male Escorts," the friendly folks at Google assumed I was an amorous stud looking to wine and dine my inamorata with dinner and a Judy Garland retrospective.

It took several clicks before I finally found what I was looking for. An outfit called Miss Emily's Escort Service. Miss Emily, according to her Web site, promised to deliver *The Perfect Gentleman for the Discriminating Woman.*

I eagerly jotted down Miss Emily's address and phone number and was just about to call her when the phone rang.

"Hey, Jaine." Patti's voice came on the line. "I read your script—"

My stomach sank. I just knew Ms. Difficult was going to hate it.

"—and I really liked what you wrote."

Well, mea culpa. I'd misjudged the dear woman. She was obviously a discerning connoisseur of fine writing.

"Yes," she said, "it's really nice. But I've decided to go in a different direction."

My stomach headed south again.

"You want a rewrite?"

"Just a little noodling."

For those of you nonwriters out there, the precise English definition of "noodling" is: *Back to Square One, Sweetie.*

"Come by the house and I'll explain what I want."

"Can't you tell me over the phone?"

"I could, but then you wouldn't have to drive halfway across town in Los Angeles traffic. What fun is that?"

Okay, so what she really said was, "I'd rather tell you in person." But I knew how Patti operated.

"Can you be here in twenty minutes?"

Only if I was Superman.

I told her I'd try my best, then hung up, muttering a string of curses.

"That woman has to be the most self-centered creature west of the La Brea Tar Pits."

Prozac looked up, affronted, from where she was lolling on my new cashmere sweater.

"Aside from you, of course, darling."

It must've been the maid's day off, because Patti's mom answered the door when I showed up at their house. A trim, surgically tightened blonde in white capris and a cleavage-exposing sweater, she had Patti's long-limbed figure and cold gray eyes. And her same charming manners.

"You with the cleaning crew?" she said, eyeing me with disdain. "Use the back entrance."

She was just about the slam the door in my face when I piped up, "I'm not with the cleaning crew. I'm Patti's writer, Jaine Austen. We went to school together."

She looked me up and down, still not terribly impressed. And then her face lit up with recognition.

"Wait a minute. Aren't you the one who fell into Principal Seawright's lap at the prom? Patti told me all about it. What a hilarious story."

I'm glad one of us thought so.

"C'mon, I'll take you to Patti."

We trooped through her House Beautiful to a sunroom in the back, and then out the French doors onto the patio.

Patti was seated at a wrought iron table with an attractive

dark-haired woman, a plate of hors d'oeuvres between them. She bit into what looked like a yummy baby lamb chop and chewed it thoughtfully.

"It's nice, Veronica," she said. "But a bit too lamb-y."

"Patti, dear," her mother interrupted. "Your writer friend is here."

Patti looked up and frowned.

"Mom, are you wearing my sweater?"

"Yes, honey. I borrowed it. I hope you don't mind."

"Of course I mind. You know I hate when you borrow my stuff without asking. You're getting it all stretched out with those silicone mountains of yours."

"Don't be silly, sweetie," her mom said, just a little too brightly. "My bust is the exact same size as yours."

She was right about that. They probably got a two-for-one special at the plastic surgeon's.

"Patti and I are the same size," she said to me with no small amount of pride. "People are always mistaking us for sisters."

"Only the ones who can't see the scars behind your ears," Patti sneered.

At that, her mom's face clouded over, and with jaw tightly clenched, she spun around and headed back to the house, her heels clacking angrily on the patio flagstones. Clearly there was not a heck of a lot of love lost in this mother–daughter relationship.

"I'll be with you in a minute, Jaine," Patti said with a dismissive wave of her hand. "As soon as I'm finished with the caterer."

I cooled my heels as she bit into a scrumptious-looking shrimp concoction, which she pronounced "too fishy." She worked her way through the rest of the hors d'oeuvres (I was so glad I'd busted a gut racing over), finding fault with most of them.

With each bite she took, the caterer's smile grew stiffer.

At last, Patti was through and the poor caterer got up to go.
"You remember everything I want?" Patti asked.

"Yes," the woman said, her smile now so brittle I was afraid her cheeks were going to crack. "The lamb not so lamby, the shrimp not so fishy, the quiche a tad less eggy, and a scooch more peanut in the satay sauce."

"Perfect!" Patti chirped.

As the caterer gathered up her platter, Patti summoned me over with a flick of her wrist.

"Jaine, you remember Veronica from Hermosa, don't you?"

I looked at the attractive woman with chestnut hair and beautiful green eyes, but I had no idea who she was.

"Jaine Austen!" The woman grinned, her smile at last genuine. "It's Veronica. Veronica Hubbard."

"Veronica?" I blinked.

Good heavens. What a change from the last time I'd seen her. Back in high school, Veronica had been a rebel grunger with spiky purple hair, decked out in black leather, her eyes rimmed with raccoon circles of mascara.

"It's me, all right."

I took in her glossy hair, fresh-scrubbed complexion, and immaculate cashmere sweater and slacks.

She sure cleaned up pretty.

"Veronica owns Hubbard's Cupboard. She caters all the stars' weddings."

First Denise, the high-powered attorney, now Veronica, Caterer to the Stars. Was I the only Hermosa High alum who was scrambling to pay the rent?

"So good to see you, Jaine. How've you been?"

"Oh, Jaine's been fabulous," Patti said with a sly grin. "Not only is she a successful writer, but she's engaged to be married to a French neurosurgeon! I can't wait to introduce him to the French ambassador. He's coming to the wedding."

"Oh, Francois doesn't speak French," I said, determined

to nip this foreign language thing in the bud. "He's of French descent, that's all. In fact, he doesn't speak a word of it."

"I'll bet," Patti smirked.

I felt like ramming a baby lamb chop up her nose.

"Well, it's great seeing you again, Jaine," Veronica said, then turned to Patti. "I'll just stop by the kitchen and check out the ovens before I go."

She shot me a sympathetic smile and scampered off to freedom.

Oh, how I envied her.

"Grab a seat," Patti said, motioning me to Veronica's recently vacated chair, "and I'll tell you about the exciting new direction I want the script to take."

I lowered myself into the hot seat, but before Patti could share her exciting new direction, the French doors opened, and her mom came out onto the patio, clearly still miffed over their earlier exchange.

"The models are here to interview for the part of your bridesmaid."

"Would you believe I have to hire somebody to be my bridesmaid?" Patti said with a put-upon sigh. "I could just kill Cheryl for gaining so much weight. Take down their names, Mom. And make sure they're all size 2."

"Do it yourself, Patti. I'm not your secretary. And from now on, answer your own goddamn doorbell."

And with that, she flounced back into the house.

"Mommie Dearest," Patti said with a roll of her eyes. "You'd think nobody ever answered a door before."

Then she took my script out from under the pitcher where she'd been using it as a coaster for her iced tea.

"Like I said on the phone, your script was fine, but I've decided to take it in a new direction. A little less *Friends*. A little more *Grey's Anatomy*."

Grey's Anatomy??? What the heck did that mean? Did she want a wedding, or an appendectomy?

"The *Friends* approach was sweet, but I want to capture the sexual tension between the doctors."

I was back on Auto Nod as she nattered on about turning Dickie into Dr. McDreamy. At this point, Veronica's assignment of making lamb "less lamby" was beginning to look like a cakewalk.

"You understand what I want?" she asked when she finally finished yakking.

"Sure," I lied.

"I need it ASAP."

"All righty," I said, getting up and inching toward the French doors. "I'm on it."

I was just about to make a break for it when she got that nasty glint in her eye I'd come to dread, the same look Prozac gets when she's about to pounce on my panty hose.

"You and your neurosurgeon still coming to the wedding?" she asked, her voice dripping with sarcasm.

"Of course."

"Something hasn't come up to make you cancel? An out-of-town medical conference, maybe?"

She was *thisclose* to snickering.

"I told you we'll be there, Patti. And I meant it."

"In that case," she said, whipping out a thick sheaf of papers from a stack on the table, "here's where I'm registered. I know you and 'Francois' will want to get me a gift."

Oh, great. Now I was going to have to use part of my paycheck—the same paycheck I was sweating blood for—to buy this dreadful woman a gift. Argggh.

I grabbed her stupid registry and headed back inside to the sunroom, where I saw a row of models seated on a rattan sofa. The "bridesmaids," I presumed.

One of them, a reedy blonde with a Scandinavian accent, asked, "Can we go in now?"

"Not if you value your sanity."

Can't say I didn't warn them.

* * *

I was just about to head out the front door when I heard someone call my name.

"Hey, Jaine. Wait up."

It was Veronica, hurrying toward me with her hors d'oeuvre plate under her arm.

"Can you believe Patti? What a bridezilla, huh?"

"King Kong with highlights."

"I'm on my fifth round of hors d'oeuvres," she said as we walked outside together. "But she's paying me through the nose. I couldn't afford to say no."

"I guess that's how she ropes in all her employees."

"I actually heard her tell the florist that the roses didn't smell 'rose-y' enough," she said, shaking her head in disbelief.

"I wonder if Dickie knows what he's getting himself into."

"I doubt it. Poor guy is blinded by love. Or lust. Or something. I was there when he and Patti reconnected, you know."

"You were at the reunion?"

"Yes," she nodded. "I don't usually go to those things. Why stir up miserable memories? But last year, curiosity got the better of me, and I made an appearance. I was talking to Dickie and Normalynne when Patti showed up, in full-tilt sex kitten mode. She had on a beaded turquoise gown, really short and tight, that left nothing to the imagination. Dickie took one look at her, and it was all over for Normalynne."

"Poor Normalynne," I sighed.

"Poor Dickie."

Our little chat was interrupted just then by a Rolls-Royce pulling up in the driveway.

"Patti's stepfather, Conrad Devane," Veronica whispered, as an immaculately groomed man with a deep tan and graying-at-the-temples hair stepped out of the car. "He's some kind of home builder. Makes more money than God."

"I can believe it," I said, eyeing his suit, a three-piece number that looked like it was hand-tailored for British royalty.

"Good afternoon, ladies!"

He waved genially as he headed into the house.

"He seems nice," I said.

"He is." Veronica replied. "The only nice one in the family."

"Probably because he's not a blood relative."

"Yeah. Way too many sharks in that gene pool."

"Well, good luck," I said.

"You, too."

Then we bid each other good-bye and got in our cars, happy to be heading out of shark-infested waters.

Chapter 5

Dreading the task of turning Romeo into Dr. McDreamy, I decided to procrastinate with a visit to Miss Emily's Escort Service.

Unlike my usual methods of procrastination—daytime TV, computer solitaire, and partying with my good buddies Ben & Jerry—this really wasn't a waste of time. After all, the wedding was mere days away and I hadn't even begun to line up a suitable neurosurgeon fiancé.

So after a quick pit stop at my apartment for lunch and a belly rub (Prozac got the belly rub; I got the lunch), I got in my Corolla and set off to go fiancé shopping.

Miss Emily's was headquartered in Culver City, a once-drab industrial part of town that has in recent years become hip and gentrified and ever so happening. Miss Emily's, however, was located in one of Culver City's few remaining drab pockets. I drove past the hip happening cafés to a block of auto body shops, where I found her tiny storefront office jammed between Big Al's Towing and the Acme Sheet Metal Company.

Miss Emily may have been discriminating about escorts, but she was clearly willing to lower her standards when it came to real estate.

I parked across the street and made my way over to the dingy office, my bad vibes strumming like a banjo. But I couldn't rush to judgment. After all, I wouldn't want anyone judging me by my office, aka my dining room table, complete with *I* ❤ *My Cat* coffee mug and said cat snoozing in my inbox.

No, I had to give Miss Emily a chance.

I stepped inside her establishment, gulping at the sight of the moth-eaten carpeting and creaky file cabinets that had doubtless been around since the McKinley administration.

In the center of the room, feet propped up on a battered metal desk, was a beefy guy with wiry black hair, making notes on a racing form.

"Yeah?" he said, glancing up, his voice a gravelly rasp.

"Um. I'm looking for Miss Emily."

He smiled, exposing a mouthful of gleaming (and, I suspect, store-bought) teeth.

"I'm Miss Emily."

As he put down his racing form, I could see that his substantial gut was encased in a tight black T-shirt, the words *Practice Makes Pervert* emblazoned across his chest.

Uh-oh. Time to skedaddle.

"I'm Rocky. I bought the business from the old bat three years ago. So what can I do for you, honey?" he asked, shooting me an oily grin.

Just tell him you've made a mistake and get the heck out of here.

"You lookin' for a fella? Sure you are. I can tell by that desperate look in your eye."

It's not desperation. It's nausea!

"Well, you've come to the right place," he said, bounding out from behind the desk and putting a hammy arm around my shoulder. "Trust me. I'll find you a fella that'll knock your panties off."

"You don't understand. That's not what I'm looking for—"

"You into girls? I can do that, too."

"No. No girls!"

"Here, doll, have a seat." He swept some X-rated magazines from a battered lawn chair and eased me down into it. "My clients don't usually come down here in person. Usually the gals pick their dates over the phone."

He plopped down on the edge of his desk, legs crossed (thank heavens for that), and smiled his idea of an avuncular smile, exposing a hunk of cottage cheese between his teeth.

"So, sweetie. Tell Uncle Rocky what you want."

Oh, well. As long as I was here, why not go through with it? After all, what did I have to lose—other than my appetite?

"Actually, I need somebody to be my fiancé at a wedding."

"Oh. I get it," he said with a most appalling wink. "You're the bride. He's the groom. A little game of Honeymoon Hotel, huh?"

"No, that's not it. I want somebody to pretend to be my fiancé at a real wedding."

"No hanky-panky?"

"No hanky-panky."

"Well, that's a new one," he said, shaking his head in wonder. "When you see the guys I've got on file, maybe you'll change your mind. Scandinavian Studs. Latin Lovers. Denzel Washington look-alikes. I got 'em all. Here, let me show you."

He hustled over to a battered file cabinet and pulled out some files.

"Gorgeous, huh?" he said, handing me an 8 x 10 glossy of one of his escorts.

Rocky did not lie. The guy *was* gorgeous. Forty years ago when the faded picture had no doubt been taken. By now he was probably showing up for dates on a walker.

"Or how about Alonzo?" he said, flashing another photo in front of me. "Ignore those numbers on the bottom. I'm just using his mug shot until his professional photos are ready."

"Actually, Rocky, I'm not sure this is such a good idea."

"Don't be silly, sweetheart. Of course it is. All the top movie stars come to Miss Emily when they want a date. Cameron. Julia. Angelina. And politicians, too. You ever hear of Maggie Thatcher?"

"The ex-prime minister of Great Britain?"

He nodded solemnly. "I can't say any more. I've signed a secrecy agreement. Let's just say that Maggie was one hot crumpet!"

Okay, this had been a mistake. Major mistake. I'd just tell Patti the truth, that I was single and manless and quite happy, thank you very much, to be living alone and single with my cat.

And I was just about to do so when the door opened and in walked Francois.

Actually, his name turned out to be Brad, but I swear, he was a neurosurgeon fiancé straight out of central casting. Tall and slim, with a mane of thick black hair and the chiseled cheekbones of a runway model. True, he wasn't the kind of guy I'd fall for in real life. In real life, I tend to go for sweet and vulnerable as opposed to drop-dead gorgeous. But this wasn't real life. This was a lie I was living. Of monumental proportions. I might as well go for broke and show up at the wedding with a stunner. Patti and Denise would swoon in their size 2s when they saw him.

"I'll take that one," I blurted out, like I was choosing a cookie at Mrs. Fields. "How much?"

"Oh, Brad." Rocky's smile got a whole lot oilier. "He's top of the line. He's three hundred."

"Three hundred dollars?" I gulped. That was about $250 more than I'd planned to spend.

"An hour," he added. "First hour in advance."

Aw, what the heck? This guy looked like he was worth it. I could do it under an hour. I'd have him meet me at the wedding, introduce him to Patti, and then make some excuse about why we had to leave.

I turned to Brad.

"Do you think you could pass yourself off as a doctor?"

"Of course," he said, beaming me a most winning smile. "I'm an actor."

Thank heavens this was Los Angeles, where nine out of ten beautiful people are actors!

I asked him a few questions about himself and he seemed to be able to string together a complete sentence with ease. In fact, he was a lot more articulate than most doctors I'd been to.

"So how about it, sweetheart?" Rocky grinned. "Do we have ourselves a deal?"

I got out my checkbook and started writing.

On my way home I stopped off at The Cookerie, a nose-bleed expensive kitchen supply store in Beverly Hills, to pick up a wedding gift for Patti. I chose the least expensive gift on her registry—a $90 corkscrew. Can you believe there are people in this world who spend ninety bucks for a corkscrew? Haven't they ever heard of screw top wine?

A snooty blond salesclerk rang up my purchase.

"You're giving *this* as a wedding gift? A crummy cork-screw?"

Okay, what she really said was *Cash or Charge?*, but I could read the subtitles.

But I didn't care what she or anybody else thought of me. So what if my gift was the cheapest one at the wedding? My fiancé, at least, would be the hottest.

Chapter 6

I spent the next few days frantically faxing Patti different versions of the script. I rewrote *Romeo and Juliet* as Seinfeld and Elaine, as Ray and Debra Romano, as Lucy and Ricky Ricardo. Okay, I exaggerate. But not by much. Finally, when I was pulling out my hair at the roots, Patti told me she'd decided to go back to Shakespeare's Elizabethan English—that she wanted to be "true to the times."

At this stage of the game I didn't give a flying frisbee what this maniac wanted. I tossed a few "haths" and "thees" in my original script and faxed it to her. Five minutes later she called me, and miracle of miracles: She actually liked it. I was free at last!

Well, not quite.

"I want you to come the wedding rehearsal tomorrow," she commanded, "in case there are any last-minute tweaks."

Oh, for crying out loud. Enough was enough. No way was I going to her stupid wedding rehearsal. With all the versions of the scripts I'd sent her, I'd more than earned my salary. If she wanted any tweaks, she could write them herself. I'd just tell her No, plain and simple.

Yeah, right. You know me, the original spineless wonder. The words that actually came out of my mouth were, "Sure, Patti. No problem."

* * *

When I stepped out onto the Devane patio the next day, the air was filled with the sounds of hammering and power drills. I looked over and saw a small army of workmen installing a massive party tent on the grounds behind the pool.

Off to the side, on the velvety green lawn beneath the balcony, a few rows of white wooden folding chairs had been set up for the wedding rehearsal. And scattered across the lawn were those statues of Cupid Patti said she'd be ordering—chubby marble cherubs with bare bottoms and arrows poised in the air.

Which just goes to show that all the money in the world can't buy good taste.

Denise was sitting on one of the folding chairs, chatting with the bridesmaid-for-hire, the lovely Swedish model I'd seen the other day. Cheryl sat next to them, having traded her polyester sweats for a polyester pantsuit, staring glumly into space. What, I wondered, was she doing here, after having been so unceremoniously banished from the wedding party?

Across the aisle, Dickie chatted with a stunning man, a bronzed Adonis of breathtaking proportions. For a fleeting instant, I wondered if Patti had ordered a best man to go with her bridesmaid-for-hire.

Seated next to Dickie was a middle-aged couple. I could tell right away they were his parents. Mainly because I heard him call them "Mom" and "Dad."

Dickie's father was an older version of Dickie. Same wide smile, same lanky physique. His mother, a stocky woman with a round face and thick blunt-cut graying hair, sat with her arms crossed tightly over her chest, her jaw clenched. Like Cheryl, she did not seem to be the happiest of campers.

I started across the lawn to join the wedding party when Patti suddenly came storming out of the tent, followed by her mother and stepfather.

"This is impossible!" she screamed, heading in my direction.

Oh, phooey. She wasn't happy with the script! Bridezilla wanted another rewrite.

I seriously considered turning around and making a break for it, to hell with the three grand, when I heard her whine:

"Damn those workmen. They should've been finished hours ago. We can't have a rehearsal with that racket going on."

Her stepfather put a comforting arm around her. "Now, honey," I heard him say, "the guys are almost done. They'll be gone before you know it."

"Yes, don't be such a drama queen," her mother said.

"Look who's talking," Patti snapped. "You have a fit if your Botox shots are five minutes late."

"How many times do I have to tell you?" her mother said. "They're not Botox shots. They're allergy injections!"

"In your forehead?"

"C'mon, girls." Her stepfather stepped between them, eager to avert a battle. "Let's say hello to Dickie's parents."

By now the three of them were standing just inches away from me. I froze in position, like a squirrel caught poaching a tomato, afraid Patti would notice me and spew her spleen in my direction.

But fortunately Patti's attention had now shifted to Dickie's mom.

"Damn that Eleanor," she hissed, staring at the stocky woman with the blunt cut hair. "She's still got that repulsive mole on her face. I told her to have it removed for the wedding photos, but did she do it? Nooo. She left it on, just to spite me."

Good heavens. Patti had actually asked her prospective mother-in-law to have a mole removed for the wedding! If nothing else, that alone secured her a place of honor in the Bridezilla Hall of Fame.

"Well, I'm not going to put her picture in the album," she pouted. "I refuse to have moles in my wedding memories."

"Be reasonable, Patti," her stepfather said. "You can't expect somebody to have plastic surgery just for your wedding."

"And why the hell not? I did."

"Don't try to reason with her, Conrad," her mother said. "She's impossible."

"Now, Daphna," he chided his wife, "Patti's under a lot of stress. C'mon, Patti, honey. Let's go talk to the Potters. You've got to, sooner or later."

"Oh, all right."

And so the happy family made their way to their future in-laws.

I was just allowing myself to breath normally again when I saw Veronica hurrying out from the tent.

"Hi," she said, trotting to my side. "I was checking out the tent for tomorrow when Hurricane Patti whirled in."

"Would you believe she asked Dickie's mom to have a mole removed for the wedding photos?"

"That's nothing. She asked the florist to spray perfume on the flowers to make them smell rosier."

"Amazing."

"Have you met Reverend Gorgeous yet?" Veronica nodded in the direction of the bronze Adonis I'd seen earlier, now chatting with Patti's mom.

"That's the minister?" I blinked in disbelief.

"I run into him all the time. He does all the celebrity weddings."

"I'll bet it's Standing Room Only at his sermons."

Daphna Devane was flirting with him shamelessly, practically throwing her panties at him, totally oblivious to her husband. I could picture Patti, in ten years time—heck, in ten minutes time—doing the same thing in front of Dickie.

"Well, I'd better make tracks," Veronica said, "before Patti sees me and decides she wants to change the menu again."

I watched with envy as she hurried off to freedom, then slipped into the last row of folding chairs.

Patti had wormed her way between Dickie and his mom. She sat with her back to her future mother-in-law, pointedly ignoring her, whispering in Dickie's ear, passing the time until the hammering stopped.

At last it did, and workmen began streaming out of the tent.

"Look, Patti," Conrad said. "They're leaving."

"It's about time," Patti huffed, getting up. "Let's get this show on the road. Is everybody here?"

She looked around, and her face clouded over.

"Where the hell is the best man?"

At that very moment, as if on cue, a skinny shrimp of a guy came running out of the house.

"Walter!" Patti screeched. "Where the hell have you been?"

Oh, gulp. It was Walter Barnhardt. Dickie's best friend from Hermosa High. I should've guessed he'd be Dickie's best man. They'd been buddies since kindergarten.

I slumped down in my seat, hoping Walter wouldn't spot me. All through high school, he had the most unshakable crush on me. I'd find him lurking in stairwells between classes waiting for me to appear. The minute he saw me, he'd cling to me like a human fungus, regaling me with the latest news flashes from his math club or chem lab.

He was constantly asking me to his house to see his ant farm, and I was constantly telling him that he was a very nice guy but I wasn't interested. After a while, I started leaving out the part about him being a nice guy, but that didn't stop him.

Now he was stammering excuses to Patti about being held up in traffic.

"Oh, who cares why you're late?" she snapped, cutting him off. "I'm going up to the balcony."

As Patti hurried into the house, Walter crept to a seat next to Dickie, and I breathed a sigh of relief. Thank goodness he hadn't seen me.

A few pleasant Patti-less minutes passed, and then she made her appearance on the balcony.

"Okay, I'm ready," she hollered down. "Let's do it!"

Dickie got up and stood next to one of the cupids on the lawn below her.

"Stand closer to the statue, honey," Patti cooed from above. "It symbolizes our undying love."

Where's a barf bag when you need one?

They proceeded to recite my bowdlerized balcony scene from *Romeo and Juliet*, wherein Patti gets the brilliant idea to get married here and now, thereby doing away with those pesky extra acts of the original play. Then she leaned over and blew her beloved a kiss to seal the deal. Minutes later, she came skipping out of the house and embraced Dickie for a big steamy smacker.

When they finally came up for air, she glared at her ragtag audience.

"You're supposed to be applauding."

As we clapped feebly, she and Dickie made their way up the aisle, where they then proceeded to come right back down again—Dickie with his mom, Patti with her stepfather.

Finally, flanked by their wedding party, the happy couple stood before the minister to the stars and ran through their actual wedding vows, a treacly bit of pap written by Patti that made the scribes at Hallmark look like Ezra Pound.

At last the rehearsal was over, and I began easing my way toward the house. I was determined to make my escape before Patti could ambush me with any surprise "tweaks."

I didn't get very far when I heard someone calling my name. I turned and saw Patti's stepfather hurrying to my side.

"We haven't been formally introduced," the dashing sixty-something said. "I'm Conrad Devane. I just wanted to tell you what a wonderful job you did on the script."

"Thank you."

At last. Someone in the family had said something pleasant to me.

"I hope Patti wasn't too demanding," he said with an apologetic smile.

Not any more than your average third-world despot.

"Not at all," I managed to lie.

"Please don't hurry off. We're having a little cocktail party before the rehearsal dinner, and we'd love you to join us."

And put myself in Patti's line of fire? Not on your life.

"No, thank you. I couldn't possibly. I'm not dressed for a party."

"Don't worry about that. Everyone's going to be casual."

"No, really, I can't."

"You don't want to miss out on any of Veronica's delicious hors d'oeuvres, do you?"

Oh, damn. Why did he have to go and mention hors d'oeuvres? Along with appetizers, entrées, side dishes, and desserts, hors d'oeuvres happen to be one of my favorite food courses.

"I tasted her crab-stuffed mushrooms," he said, "and they're out of this world."

Crab-stuffed mushrooms? C'mon, I'm only human.

So, throwing caution—and sanity—to the winds, I said, "Sure, why not?"

I was about to find out exactly why not, because just then I saw Walter Barnhardt sprinting across the lawn to join us.

"Jaine!" he beamed. "I thought that was you!"

Poor Walter. Whereas Dickie had blossomed into a stud-muffin, Walter had remained firmly entrenched in the Valley of the Nerds. If anything, he'd grown nerdier. His ears seemed to stick out farther than they had in high school, as did his teeth.

And to top things off—literally—he was sporting the ghastliest wig I'd ever seen outside of a Halloween party.

"Are you staying for cocktails?" he asked.

"Of course she is," Conrad said. "She just told me she would."

"Super!" Walter said, eyeing me like a starving dog who's just been handed a T-bone.

Chapter 7

It turns out I had totally misjudged Walter. I just assumed by the creepy way he'd clung to me like lichen in high school that he was a painfully awkward geekazoid. I couldn't have been more wrong. Now that I finally got a chance to talk with him, I discovered he was a painfully obnoxious geekazoid.

The guy never shut up. He had me trapped in a dim corner of the party, blocking my escape, while he rattled on about his colorful life as an insurance actuary.

I tried not to stare at the god-awful nest of hair perched on his head like a dead hamster. I wondered if it had come with a rabies shot.

"Want to know your odds of getting killed by decapitation?" he asked cheerfully.

"Who doesn't?"

Having failed to detect the irony in my reply, he was off and running with a bunch of gruesome statistics. Actually, at this point, the idea of death by decapitation was beginning to have a certain appeal. At the very least, it would put an end to this conversation.

What really got me was that while I was trapped with the Human Actuarial Table, I could see Veronica and her wait staff circulating around the room with trays of divine smelling hors d'oeuvres. I tried to signal them, but they didn't notice me tucked away in this godforsaken corner.

At last, Walter stopped yapping about his job and flashed me what he probably thought was a sexy grin.

"So, Jaine. I don't see any ring on your finger. I guess that means you must be single."

"Actually, Walter, I'm engaged."

"You are?" He blinked in amazement.

I couldn't help but feel a tad irritated. What was so damn surprising about me having a guy in my life?

"Yes. My fiancé will be coming to the wedding tomorrow."

Thank heavens for Miss Emily aka Rocky and the fabulous Brad aka Francois. Maybe telling Patti and Denise that whopper of a lie wasn't such a stupid move after all.

Walter gulped, disappointed, and I took advantage of the momentary lull in the conversation to make my getaway.

"Well, it's been fun chatting," I said, practically burning rubber as I bolted to freedom.

By now the Devanes' "little" party was wall-to-wall guests. Patti sashayed among them, arm in arm with Dickie, showing him off like a trinket she'd picked up at Neiman's. Her stepfather, engrossed in conversation with another captain of industry, didn't seem to notice or care that his wife was flirting shamelessly with the hunky reverend.

I joined the revelers and scooted over to Veronica, who was weaving her way among the partygoers in her chef's jacket, holding a tray of those crab-stuffed mushrooms Conrad had touted. I grabbed one and gobbled it down. Sheer heaven.

"Have another," Veronica urged. "All the skinny minnies here are afraid to eat anything more fattening than a celery stick."

So I took another. And, if you must know, another.

"How come you're out here serving?" I asked, between bites. "Shouldn't you be in the kitchen?"

"Yes, I should, but Patti sent home one of my waiters. She said his red hair clashed with her dress."

"You're kidding, right?"

"I wish I were," she sighed. "Hey, it looks like you're about to have company."

She nodded in the direction of Walter, who was making his way across the room.

"Quick, where's the bathroom?"

"Down the hall to your right."

"Thanks."

Grabbing one more mushroom for the road, I dashed down the hallway and ducked into the first room I saw.

It was not a bathroom, but a library of some sort, decorated in tufted Gentleman's Club leather and hunting prints. What riveted my attention, however, was not the plush upholstery or the Currier & Ives prints—but Cheryl, sprawled out on the sofa, a bottle of champagne balanced on her tummy.

"C'mon in," she said, waving me inside. "Want some champagne?"

She held out the bottle.

"No, thanks."

Call me wacky, but I prefer my bubbly sans spit.

"I stole it from behind the bar," she giggled. "I figured I deserved it for sitting through that stupid rehearsal."

She raised the bottle to her lips and took a healthy slug.

"I still can't believe I drove all the way up here to watch that nonsense. But Patti insisted. Said she didn't want me to miss out on any of the fun. Hah! She just wanted me to feel like a fat fool while that skinny Swedish chick paraded around in my place. I should've told her to take her stupid wedding and blow it out her liposuctioned fanny."

She held up the champagne bottle in a mock toast.

"Here's to the bride. May she get herpes on her honeymoon."

She took another slug of the bubbly and wiped her mouth with the back of her hand.

"Hey, why don't we go back to the party and grab some hors d'oeuvres?" I suggested, thinking it would be wise to put something else in her system other than alcohol.

But Cheryl wasn't listening.

"The miserable bitch," she muttered, lost in thoughts of Patti. "She ruined my life."

"The crab-stuffed mushrooms are fabulous," I said, wondering how Patti had ruined Cheryl's life.

Cheryl looked up, a flicker of interest in her glazed blue eyes.

"Crab-stuffed mushrooms, huh?"

"They're really good."

Then she eyed her champagne.

"Nah," she said, succumbing to the lure of the bubbly. "I think I'll stay here."

"Well, it was nice running into you," I offered lamely as I headed for the door.

"Jaine," she called out from the depths of the sofa.

I turned to face her.

"Yes?"

"I'm sorry I was so nasty to you in high school."

"You weren't so bad."

"Oh, yes, I was," she sighed. "And I'm paying for it now. I'm utterly miserable, if that's any consolation."

"It's no consolation, Cheryl," I said, meaning it. "I hope things get better for you. Just take it easy on that champagne, okay?"

"Sure," she said, once more putting the bottle to her lips.

I dreaded to think of the sparks that would fly if Patti discovered Cheryl snockered under the Currier & Ives.

But when I got back to the party I saw that Patti was somewhat tootled herself.

As I stood in the entrance to the living room, she was still making the rounds of the party, her arm hooked proprietarily through Dickie's. She stopped to chat with Denise and her significant other, a sleek bizguy who looked like he just stepped out of a Rolex ad.

"You guys having fun?" Patti asked, her voice loud and a bit slurred.

"Of course," Denise replied. "We're having a lovely time."

"Not as much fun as last night, huh?" Patti said with a broad wink. "That was some bachelorette party. Did we get wasted or what?"

Denise nodded, smiling stiffly.

"We went to a male strip club," Patti informed Mr. Rolex. "Talk about your hunk heaven, huh, Denise?"

Denise offered another stiff smile. Clearly it had not been not her idea of a fun evening.

"But none of the strippers were as hot as my Dickie," Patti said, nuzzling Dickie's neck with a kiss.

Dickie blushed, both embarrassed and pleased.

It was then that I heard someone hiss:

"Drunken slut."

I turned and saw Dickie's parents standing not far from me. Mrs. Potter's jaw was clenched tight with disgust.

"I can't let him go through with it, Kyle."

"Take it easy, Eleanor," her husband said, putting his arm around her.

She jerked away from his touch.

"Don't try to pacify me. Can't you see what's happening? Dickie's nothing but a toy to her. Her latest plaything. She'll be cheating on him before the ink on the marriage license is dry."

Her husband sighed.

"Just look at the way her mother is flirting with the minister. Like mother, like daughter. Sluts, both of them."

"Try not to worry, dear. Everything's going to be okay."

"You bet things are going to be okay," Eleanor Potter said, her eyes steely with determination. "That bitch is not going to be my daughter-in-law. I'm going to see to that."

"Eleanor, hush." Her husband, having spotted me eaves-dropping, gestured in my direction.

I smiled weakly and backed out into the hallway.

Oh, well. It was time I left the party anyway. As much as I would've liked to nab some more hors d'oeuvres, I couldn't risk running into Walter.

So I made my way to the front door, wondering exactly what Eleanor Potter planned to do to stop Patti from becoming her daughter-in-law.

I was just about to let myself out when I heard Patti calling my name.

"Jaine, wait."

I turned and saw her coming out into the foyer.

"Before you leave," she chirped, "I've got something for you."

My paycheck! O blessed day!

"Wait here. I'll be right back."

Well, wasn't that a happy surprise? I thought for sure she'd be one of those clients who kept me waiting for weeks before coughing up my pay.

Minutes later she came back—alas, paycheck-free. The only thing she had in her hot little hands was her dog, Mamie, whiter and fluffier than ever, with a pink polka-dot bow in her hair.

"Look who just came back from the groomers," Patti cooed. "Doesn't she look gorgeous?"

"Gorgeous," I echoed, a stiff smile plastered on my face.

"She's going to be Flower Dog at the wedding tomorrow."

"Flower Dog?"

Now I'd heard everything.

"Yes, she's going to walk down the aisle with a basket of rose petals in her little mouth."

Poor Mamie. I could only imagine what nonsense she had to put up with. I was surprised she wasn't wearing thong underwear and hair extensions.

"Anyhow, I was wondering if you could do me a teeny tiny favor and keep her at your place tonight."

My place? Was she nuts?

"We're all heading off to the rehearsal dinner, and I hate leaving her home alone."

"What about your maid? Won't she be here?"

"Oh, Mamie doesn't like to be with servants. She wants to hang out with real people. Isn't that right, sweetheart?"

Real people?? Alert the media. Marie Antoinette was alive and well in Bel Air.

"You don't mind, do you?" she said, thrusting the dog in my arms.

"Actually, Patti, I don't think it's such a good idea."

The dog began licking my face, having picked up the scent of crab-stuffed mushrooms.

"Of course it is. Look how she adores you."

"But, Patti. I've got a cat."

"No problem. Mamie hardly ever bites."

The next thing I knew, she was handing me a Neiman Marcus shopping bag.

"Here are her toys and food. She's on a special diet."

"But—"

"Keep her at your place tomorrow morning. I don't want her underfoot while I'm getting dressed. Just bring her back about a half hour before the ceremony."

Before I could voice any further objections, she was skipping back to the party.

"And don't forget to bring that fabulous fiancé of yours!"

Then, flapping her fingers in a dismissive wave, she disappeared into the crowd.

I looked down at the bundle of white fluff in my arms, and a rush of sympathy washed over me. Like Dickie, poor Mamie was undoubtedly Patti's Plaything du Jour. As soon as the dog got old and arthritic, her eyes clouded with cataracts, no longer a cute accessory, she'd be history.

"Okay, Mamie," I sighed, stepping outside. "Ready to go slumming?"

Chapter 8

I drove home with Mamie in the backseat. She was having the time of her life, racing back and forth from one side of the car to the other, not wanting to miss one palm tree or street lamp.

My state of mind, however, was a tad less jubilant. I'd been insane to take her, of course. I fully expected World War III to break out the minute Prozac set eyes on her. Prozac likes being an only child.

But their meeting, much to my relief, was surprisingly uneventful.

Not that Prozac was happy about having a houseguest. Not one bit. The minute she saw Mamie, her eyes narrowed in disgust.

What's THAT doing here?

"This is Mamie, darling. She's just staying for one night. You don't mind, do you?"

Get a clue, Sherlock. What do you think?

If she had fingers, I'm sure she would've given me one.

I put Mamie down to see how the two would interact, fully prepared to snatch one of them up at the first sign of trouble.

But there was no bloodshed. No fur flew. On the contrary, Mamie scampered over to Prozac and began sniffing her amiably, eager to be friends.

"See?" I said. "She likes you."

Of course she likes me. What's not to like? Just tell Fluffy here the feeling isn't mutual.

She bared her teeth in a most unfriendly hiss.

I guess Mamie got the hint because she abandoned Prozac and began sniffing my hardwood floors with all the intensity of Long John Silver in search of buried treasure.

I, meanwhile, started unpacking her toys—a veritable Santa's workshop of balls, bells, and stuffed animals. Not to mention a stuffed toy violin that actually played music, and a cell phone that actually rang.

Prozac gazed at the display through slitted eyes.

Jeez. Fluff-O gets enough toys to stock a Toys "R" Us, and all I get is a crummy rubber mouse.

Having sniffed her way around the room, Mamie now scampered back to join us.

"Hey, Mamie," I said, picking up her cell phone. "Want to check your messages?"

But Mamie wasn't interested in her toys. She went right back to Prozac, panting wetly.

Prozac eyed her with disgust.

Take a hike, Cottonball.

And in one fluid movement, Prozac slithered down off the sofa, across the room, and up onto the top of the bookshelf, where she gazed down imperiously at us peasants below.

Wake me when she's gone.

"Oh, Pro. Don't be that way."

But she was going to be that way. With a final hiss, she curled up in a ball and turned her back on us. The cold shoulder treatment had officially begun.

I tried in vain to tempt her with dinner, but when I opened a can of Minced Mackerel Guts—a sound that normally sends her barreling to the kitchen at the speed of light—there were no little paws thundering across the linoleum.

"Looks like it's just you and me, kid," I said to Mamie,

reaching into the Neiman Marcus bag to get her dog food. Imagine my surprise when I pulled out a tupperware container filled with tiny cubes of cut-up steak. And not the broiled hockey pucks I get at Sizzler either. This was filet mignon. I happen to know this for a fact because I helped myself to a couple of bites.

Yes, I know I should be ashamed of myself, mooching off a dog's dinner, but I couldn't resist. Besides I had only two or three tiny pieces. (Okay, five.)

And Mamie didn't seem to mind. In fact, she seemed quite taken with me. Ever since Prozac had retired to the bookshelf, Mamie had been following me around, staring up at me with worshipful eyes.

"Okay, sweetie," I said, bending down to give her a love scratch. "Time for your dinner."

I put some of her steak in a plastic bowl—why did I get the feeling she was used to eating off Limoges?—and set it down in front of her.

Unlike Prozac, who attacks her food with all the gusto of a longshoreman at a truck stop café, Mamie nibbled at hers daintily.

I watched with envy as she ate the succulent morsels.

With a sigh, I began scrounging around my barren cupboards to fix something for my own dinner. I finally rustled up some mini-tuna sandwiches on Saltines. Accompanied by a side of canned beets. One of these days, I really had to stock up on staples.

After dinner, I took Mamie for a walk. Her little nose went into overdrive, sniffing at every patch of grass and tree in sight, getting acquainted with her new neighborhood. Finally she settled on a lush patch of lawn in front of a neighboring duplex and left a poop the size of a Junior Mint. I scooped it into a baggie, although I doubted anyone would have noticed it, not without a microscope.

Back home, I tried to interest her in her toys again, but she only had eyes for me. All she wanted was to sit in my lap and stare up at me worshipfully.

Why couldn't Prozac ever show me devotion like this? No wonder dog people were so crazy about their dogs.

I tried several times to coax Prozac down from the bookshelf, but she wouldn't budge.

Oh, well, I told myself, as I got in bed and turned on the TV, Mamie would be gone tomorrow and Prozac would be back on the couch and eating like a sumo wrestler.

I spent the next couple of hours watching *Rear Window*, with Mamie curled at my feet. When it was over, I turned out the light to go to sleep. But sleep didn't come. Sleep never comes easily without Prozac nestled in the crook of my neck.

I was just about to get out of bed and grovel for her forgiveness when she sauntered into the bedroom.

With a single graceful leap she was on the bed.

Mamie, who knew better than to try anything stupid like joining us for a lick and sniff session, stayed put at the foot of the bed.

"Oh, Prozac. I missed you!" I took her in my arms and began stroking her. "Did you eat your mackerel guts?"

She yawned a cavernous yawn, sending a blast of mackerel fumes in my direction.

"I'll take that as a yes."

Then we curled up together, Prozac nestled in her usual position in the crook of my neck. And as I felt her warm body purring against mine, I finally relaxed.

No wonder cat people are so crazy about their cats.

I woke up the next morning, sun streaming in my bedroom window. I checked my clock radio and saw that ~~that~~ it was after nine. Prozac, the little angel, had let me sleep in for a change.

I stretched lazily in bed. The wedding wasn't until two that afternoon and I still had the whole morning to get spiffed up.

I intended to give myself the works: manicure, pedicure, leg wax, eyebrow pluck. I'd luxuriate in a delicious bubble bath, after which I'd blow-dry my stubborn curls to silky perfection and slip into a slinky black cocktail dress I'd bought a couple of months ago, the only item to have escaped the wrath of Lance's Closet Makeover.

I'd tried it on the other day, and much to my amazement it hadn't shrunk in the closet like so much of my clothing tends to do. I could see myself at the wedding in my slinky dress, exfoliated and coiffed, my hunkalicious fiancé-for-hire at my side. And for the first time since this whole mess began, I had good vibes about the wedding. Maybe it wouldn't be such a disaster after all.

So it was with a spring in my step and hope in my heart that I got out of bed and headed for the kitchen to fix breakfast.

And that's where my trip to Fantasy Island came screeching to a halt.

The first thing I saw when I walked in the kitchen was my garbage can upended, its messy contents scattered on the floor.

The second thing I saw was Mamie rolling around in said garbage.

Her formerly pristine white fur was dotted with bits of tuna, low-fat mayo, petrified pizza crusts, and blobs of beet juice. All of it sprinkled with a generous coating of coffee grounds. Off to the side was a small puddle where she'd taken a tinkle.

No wonder Prozac let me sleep in; she'd masterminded this whole fiasco.

She was lolling on the kitchen counter now, with what I could swear was a smirk on her face.

"You're responsible for all this, aren't you?" I hissed.

She shot me one of her Innocent Bystander looks, the same look she gives me when I come home to find my panty hose shredded to cole slaw.

Moi?

"Oh, don't play innocent. I know you put her up to it."

Whatever. So what's for breakfast?

She jumped down from the counter and began her Feed Me dance around my ankles.

I can't believe I actually fed the little monster, but I didn't want to be tripping over her all morning.

"You don't deserve this," I said as I tossed her some Luscious Lamb Guts.

Then I gave Mamie the rest of her filet mignon. Needless to say, two seconds later, Prozac's little pink nose was buried in Mamie's dish, and poor Mamie had to settle for the lamb guts.

Meanwhile, I got down on my knees and began cleaning up the mess on the floor. I'd just wiped up the last glob of beet juice when the phone rang. Wearily I answered it.

"Hey, Jaine. It's Patti."

Oh, Lord. Not Patti. Not now.

"What's Mamie up to?"

Her neck in garbage.

"Nothing much. She's just hanging out."

"Let me speak to her."

"You want to *speak* with her?"

"Yes. Put her on the phone."

Stifling a groan, I held the receiver to Mamie's ear. She licked it eagerly as Patti cooed baby talk on the other end. After a few nauseating beats of this nonsense, I grabbed the phone back and said good-bye to Patti through a mist of lamb-scented dog spit.

Then I hung up and checked my watch. Only 9:45. No need to panic. I still had plenty of time to get Mamie groomed for the wedding.

After wiping down the receiver with Lysol, I got back on the phone and started calling dog groomers. But it was Saturday, a busy day in the pet grooming world. Every place I called was booked solid, except for one salon out in Tujunga that couldn't squeeze us in until 4:30.

Okay, then. I was just going to have to groom her myself.

I hurried to the bathroom and ran the water in the tub, adding a generous heaping of bubble bath.

The trouble came when I tried adding Mamie.

They say many dogs like baths. I can assure you Mamie wasn't one of them. From the way she carried on, you would've thought I was giving her electric shock treatments. In no time, I was drenched.

All the while Prozac gazed down at us, highly amused, from her perch atop the toilet tank.

This is more fun than watching you try on bathing suits.

Finally, the terrible ordeal was over, and I faced the even worse ordeal of drying Mamie's hair. Ever try holding down a squirming dog with one hand and a hair dryer with the other, scrunching curly ringlets as you go?

My advice: Don't.

Never again would I complain about straightening my own mop.

At last I was finished. Mamie didn't look quite as fluffy as she'd looked yesterday, but it would have to do. As she dashed off to freedom, I checked the time. Still hours till the wedding. If I took a quick shower, I'd have plenty of time to wax my legs and do my nails and blow my hair straight.

And then I remembered: Mamie's pink polka-dot hair bow!

I raced to the kitchen and fished it out from where I'd tossed it in the garbage. I groaned at the sight of it—reeking of tuna and stained purple with beet juice.

I tried scrubbing it with Wisk, but the stains—and the stink—were set for life.

Damn. I was going to have to buy another one.

Muttering a steady stream of curses, I changed out of my soggy pajamas into a pair of sweats, then headed out to my

Corolla with Mamie in my arms. No way was I going to leave her alone with the she-devil Prozac.

After plopping her alongside me in the passenger seat, I strapped myself in and set off to go bow hunting.

Do you realize how tough it is to find a pink polka-dot hair bow? Trust me, Columbus had less trouble finding America.

I spent the next two hours fruitlessly driving from one beauty supply store to another. I saw more hair accessories that day than I'd seen in my entire life. It was in Nordstrom's Children's department that I finally found a reasonable facsimile of the bow. It was more dusty rose than pink, and the polka dots were a little too big, but it was better than nothing. I just prayed Patti wouldn't look at Mamie too closely.

By the time I got home with my treasure, my hours of prep time were gone with the wind. I was supposed to be at Patti's house in twenty minutes. Which left me exactly zero time to do any personal grooming.

I threw on my dress and lassoed my unruly curls in a scrunchy, all thoughts of looking spiffy flying out the window.

Oh, well, I reminded myself. All was not lost. So what if I looked less than wonderful? I still had Brad, my hunkalicious fiancé, didn't I?

The answer to that rhetorical question, as turned out, was a resounding No.

Because just then the phone rang. I was going to let the machine get it, but when I heard Brad's voice I snatched it up.

"Jaine, I'm so sorry, but I'm not going to be able to make it to the wedding today."

"What???"

Was it possible this was all a bad dream and that any second I'd feel Prozac clawing my chest to wake me for her breakfast?

No such luck.

"My car broke down on the freeway," Brad was saying. "I'm waiting for the tow truck now. I left a message with Rocky to send somebody else to the wedding, but at this late hour, I wouldn't get your hopes up."

No need to worry about that. My hopes had just plummeted to the cellar of my psyche where they belonged.

I should've known all along I'd never be able to put one over on Patti.

Chapter 9

Feeling a lot like Cinderella's frumpy stepsister, I drove up to Patti's Bel Air estate and handed my car keys to one of the red-coated valets out front.

"You going to the Devane–Potter wedding?" he asked, clearly taking me for someone whose true destination had been the Olive Garden All You Can Eat Spaghetti & Meatball Festival.

"Unfortunately," I said, gathering up Mamie and my $90 corkscrew, "I am."

I headed to the house, where the maid I'd met on my first visit answered the door, looking like she could use a valium or three.

"Patti's upstairs in her bedroom," she said wearily. Then she skittered away, muttering under her breath. I couldn't be sure, but I thought I heard the words "loco" and "nutcase."

I tossed my corkscrew onto the mountain of wedding-white gift boxes, grateful that I'd sprung for The Cookerie's outrageous gift wrap charge. Mine might have been the cheapest gift on the registry, but from the outside, at least, it fit right in with all the others.

Then I made my way upstairs, praying Patti wouldn't notice anything amiss with Mamie.

The door to Patti's bubblegum pink bedroom was open, and I stepped tentatively inside. Patti, looking very *Shake-*

speare in Love-ish in her Renaissance-themed wedding gown, sat at her vanity, in the middle of a conversation with Veronica.

A slim male hairdresser hovered over her, separating artful tendrils from her elaborate upswept do. Denise and the Swedish bridesmaid, also dressed for a Renaissance Faire, sat nearby on Patti's pink canopy bed, following Patti's conversation with Veronica like spectators at a tennis match.

"Romaine lettuce?" Patti screeched, her nostrils flared. "I can't have romaine lettuce at my wedding!"

Veronica, in her chef's scrubs, forced a smile.

"Patti," she said, enunciating her syllables as if talking to a five-year-old, "I already explained. It was unavoidable. The frisee lettuce never showed up. We have no choice but to go with romaine."

"But I don't want romaine," Patti shrieked, swatting the hairdresser away. "I want frisee. And I want it today."

And at that moment, something in Veronica snapped.

"Oh, grow up, Patti." Anger blazed in her eyes.

"What?" Patti gasped, unused to back talk.

"Of all the impossible people I've ever worked for, and I've worked for plenty, you win, hands down. You'll get romaine and like it."

Everyone in the room—except Mamie, who was busy nibbling on my earlobe—reacted in stunned silence.

"I'm sorry I ever took this stupid job. No amount of money is worth having to put up with a prima donna like you."

"Is that so?" Patti hissed. "Well, you're going to be even sorrier when I get through with you. I happen to have a lot of influential friends in this town. And I intend to tell each and every one of them that you couldn't deliver a simple frisee salad."

"*You* have friends?" Veronica sneered. "Oh, really? Do you rent them by the hour, like your bridesmaid?"

Patti's face flushed with fury.

"You'll never cater in this town again!" she shrieked.

"Oh, Patti. Go frisee yourself," Veronica shot back, storming out of the room. Only "frisee" wasn't the "F" word she used.

The strained silence that followed her exit was broken by the appearance of Patti's mom in the doorway. Encased in a slinky tube of a dress, Daphna Devane looked more like an aging beauty pageant contestant than the mother of the bride.

"Better get a move on, Patti," she said. "The guests are starting to show up. And put some Visine in your eyes," she added before hustling off down the hallway. "They're still bloodshot from your bachelorette party."

"Thanks, Mom," Patti said to the empty space where her mother had been standing. "You look lovely, too."

It was then that she noticed me hovering by the door with Mamie in my arms.

"Mamie, precious! I didn't see you. Bring her over here, Jaine. I want to say hello to my little darling."

I crossed over to Patti with my heart in my throat, once again praying she wouldn't notice Mamie's new look.

"There you are, sweetheart!" Patti reached to get her and let out a bloodcurdling wail.

Oh, crud. She'd noticed.

So much for any letters of recommendation from Patti. I braced myself for a rousing You'll Never Work in This Town Again speech, when I realized she wasn't looking at Mamie. No, her eyes were riveted on one of her fingernails.

"Oh, God!" she wailed. "I chipped my nail! First the romaine. Now this. Why does everything always happen to me?"

Yeah, poor Job had nothing on Patti.

As the others rushed over to inspect the damage, I figured it was a good time to make myself scarce. I didn't want to be around when and if Patti got a good look at her beloved Flower Dog.

I edged for the door and was just about to step over the threshold to freedom when Patti called out to me.

"Hold on, Jaine."

"Yes?" I turned and faced her with a feeble smile.

"Where's your fiancé?" she smirked. "The neurosurgeon?"

In spite of the chipped nail and romaine tragedies, it looked like Patti still had the energy to turn the knife and make me squirm.

"Um, actually, I don't think he's going to make it," I stammered.

"I didn't think he would," Patti said, with a smug smile.

I stood there, feeling just like I felt all those years ago when Patti grilled me about my prom date. I was just about to tell her the truth, that the only doctor in my life was Dr Pepper, when I heard:

"Jaine! I'm so sorry I'm late."

I turned to see Brad, my hunkalicious paid escort, standing in the hallway.

"Br—Francois!" I gasped.

"Is that your fiancé out there?" Patti asked.

I nodded numbly.

"Well, ask him in!"

And then, in a moment I'll always treasure, Brad stepped in the room.

You should've seen the look on Patti's face. It was almost worth all the nonsense I'd put up with from her. She and Denise gaped at Brad, slack jawed. Even the Swedish model was giving him the onceover. Not to mention the hairdresser.

"Hi, darling," Brad said, brushing his lips lightly against mine.

Patti's jaw was still hanging open. Any minute now, she'd be drooling.

"Hope I'm not interrupting anything," Brad said to her.

"Not at all." Patti cooed, regaining her powers of speech.

"I would've been here sooner, but I got held up at the hospital. Finally got another surgeon to cover for me."

"How clever of you," Patti said, batting her eyelash extensions at him.

Then she turned to me, smiling sweetly for Brad's benefit.

"Jaine, darling. You sure snagged yourself a honey. Why, he's handsome as a movie star." Then, once more locking eyeballs with Brad: "Are you sure I haven't seen you up on the big screen?"

"Nope," Brad said. "The only place I perform is in the operating room."

"Well, sign me up for surgery," she said with a wink.

Hey, sweetheart. In case you forgot, you're getting married in an hour.

"Yes, Brad," Denise said, joining our little coffee klatch. "Your face looks awfully familiar. I feel like we've met before."

Oh, rats. Was my cover about to be blown? Had straight-laced Denise actually cheated on Mr. Rolex and used the services of Miss Emily?

"I know!" she beamed. "It was at the Chamber of Commerce dinner last Thursday."

"I don't think so," Brad said, putting his arm around me. "Last Thursday Jaine and I spent a quiet evening at my place. Didn't we, hon?"

He smiled at me, one of those adoring smiles men give to women in Estée Lauder ads.

"Uh-huh," I nodded, too bowled over by his magnificent performance to speak actual English.

"Well, honey," he said, "we'd better go downstairs and let Patti finish dressing."

And as he guided me out of the room, his hand draped possessively around my waist, I exulted in my moment of triumph.

This guy was worth every penny I was paying him. And then some.

"How on earth did you get here?" I asked, as Brad and I made our way downstairs.

"You won't believe what happened. Right after I got off the phone with you, a woman in a Mercedes pulled up and said she'd give me a lift."

"But what about your car? Did you just leave it on the freeway?"

"Mona—that's the woman's name—is having it towed to her mechanic, and then she's going to come back here to pick me up. I can't believe how sweet she was."

I, on the other hand, had no trouble believing it.

Brad was the kind of guy women bent over backward for. Literally and figuratively.

By now we'd made our way out back where the festivities were getting under way. A trio of musicians in Renaissance tights and puffy blouses were belting out sixteenth-century golden oldies to the assembled guests, most of whom were milling around a bar set up on the lawn.

I was surprised to see they were serving drinks before the wedding "show." Probably to numb the audience.

Breaking with wedding tradition, members of the wedding party were out among the guests. Dickie and the Devanes were making the rounds, meeting and greeting. Dickie's parents stood off to the side, his mother's face a grim mask, his father smiling nervously.

Cheryl—who, like yours truly, hadn't bothered to fix her hair or apply makeup—hovered near the bartender, guzzling from a flute of champagne. She looked up briefly when she saw Brad and me together, but she was far more interested in what the bartender had to offer, and handed him her glass for a refill.

Brad and I joined the others out on the lawn, and Dickie, catching sight of us, came over to greet us.

"So glad you could make it, Jaine."

He stood there, beaming—clean and fresh scrubbed, a tiny cowlick at the back of his head—and suddenly I wanted to warn him to make a break for it while there was still time.

But of course, I didn't. All I did was introduce him to my phony fiancé.

"You two are engaged?" he asked, unable to mask his surprise. I was beginning to feel like the Elephant Man on a date with Nicole Kidman.

"Well, that's wonderful!" he said, quickly recovering. "I hope you'll be as happy as Patti and me."

Poor innocent fool. He actually thought he had a shot at happiness.

He left us to circulate, and Brad started telling me about his life as a Miss Emily's escort (just doing it to pay the rent) and his career as an aspiring actor (someday he wants to direct, in case you're interested). We were standing there chatting when I looked up and saw Walter Barnhardt heading in our direction.

"Quick," I whispered. "Act like you're madly in love."

Instantly Brad shifted into lovebird gear, gazing into my eyes and running his finger along my cheek.

"Hello, Jaine." Walter stood in front of us, his god-awful toupee perched on his head like a dynel bird's nest.

"Oh. Hi, Walter." I pretended to notice him for the first time. "I'd like you to meet my fiancé, Francois."

"Francois?" Walter shot me a dubious look.

"Yes, Dr. Francois Cliquot," I countered, taking inspiration from a waiter toting a bottle of Veuve Cliquot.

Walter grunted a curt hello.

"You two are engaged?" he asked, a little too suspiciously for my tastes.

"For keeps," Brad said, wrapping his arm around me in a possessive hug.

"Really?" Walter said, oozing disbelief. "Somehow I can't picture the two of you together."

"Well, we are," I said defiantly.

"Nice meeting you, Walter," Brad said, dismissing him with a cool smile.

"Yeah, right."

He shuffled away, and I thought we were rid of him, but a few minutes later he was hovering behind us, nursing a Coke, pretending not to be eavesdropping. Which meant we had to spend the next fifteen minutes faking a discussion about where to go on our fictional honeymoon.

Every once in a while, we'd drift over to another part of the lawn, but sooner or later Walter would follow. It seemed as if we weren't going to be able to shake him until the ceremony began. Which, from the looks of things, might not be for a long time.

Denise and the Swedish model had joined the guests on the lawn. According to them, Patti was waiting for a manicurist to show up to fix the chip in her nail.

And so the minutes ticked by.

Around about the time I thought we'd be watching the ceremony at midnight, a parade of waiters in Renaissance garb came streaming out of the house, bearing trays of what looked like small torches.

"Attention, everybody," Conrad Devane called out. "Since Patti is taking a little longer than expected"—at which point, Daphna Devane rolled her eyes theatrically—"I want everybody to enjoy a flaming Elizabethan rum punch! It's Patti's favorite cocktail. Now don't blow out the flames until we've toasted the bride and groom."

Brad took two drinks off a passing tray and handed me one, the flames licking at my eyebrows.

Leave it to Patti to come up with a dopey drink like this.

When everyone had been served, Conrad raised his drink in a toast.

"To Patti and Dickie."

"To Patti and Dickie," we all echoed hollowly.

Denise was watching us now, and once again Brad shifted into high octane lovebird mode, staring worshipfully into my eyes and entwining his drinking arm with mine.

We were just about to blow out the flames and drink our ridiculous concoctions when a passing waiter, no doubt unused to traipsing around in tights, tripped and jostled my arm.

The poor guy apologized profusely, and I told him it was nothing to worry about.

Wrong.

There was plenty to worry about.

Because just then I smelled smoke.

I turned and, to my horror, saw that it was coming from Walter's toupee. Good heavens, I'd set Walter's hairpiece on fire!

Suddenly flames started shooting from the matted fur.

"Walter!" I screamed. "Your hair's on fire."

At which point, Brad sprang into action, whipping the wig from Walter's head and hurling it to the ground, where he proceeded to stomp out the flames.

Walter eyed the charred remains of his toupee and whirled on me, furious.

"You did this, didn't you?"

"Walter, I swear it was an accident!"

"First you reject me in high school, and now you set my hair on fire!"

I continued to protest that it had all been a ghastly accident, but I didn't get very far. Because Denise, who had been staring intently at Brad throughout this whole firefighting escapade, suddenly blurted out: "Now I know where I saw you before! At Patti's bachelorette party. You were one of the male strippers. You're Fireman Brad!"

All eyes were now on me and Brad.

He turned to me, sheepish.

"It's a part-time gig," he shrugged.

"You're engaged to a male stripper?" Walter asked.

"We're not engaged," I sighed. This stupid charade had gone on long enough. "He's not my fiancé. He's a paid escort, all right?"

"You're here with a paid escort?" Walter bellowed, just in case anybody in Pomona didn't hear.

"I'm so sorry about this, Jaine," Brad said, his eyes wide with sympathy. "But actually your hour is up, so unless you want to spring for another three hundred dollars, I'd better be going. Besides, Mona's probably waiting for me out front."

He gave me a plaintive wave good-bye and headed off, crossing paths with Conrad, who had just come from inside the house.

"Okay, everybody," Conrad said. "Grab a seat. Patti's ready now. The show's about to start."

The guests began trooping across the lawn to their seats. Nothing, I thought, could possibly top the show they'd just seen.

How wrong I was.

Chapter 10

I thought about running out after Brad, away from this ghastly wedding, but I refused to take the coward's way out. We Austens are a proud people. Instead, I took a seat on one of the white slatted folding chairs, determined to suck in my gut, hold my head high, and stuff my face with as much free food at the reception as possible.

I soon began to regret my decision. All around me, people were shooting me covert glances, whispering about the Flaming Toupee Affair.

Their whispers died down, however, when strains of lilting flute music filled the air and Patti came floating out onto the balcony, looking far lovelier than she deserved.

Dickie stood below her beside one of the Cupid statues and smiled nervously. I couldn't be sure, but I thought I saw a cheat sheet with his lines propped up on Cupid's diaper.

"Dickie, Dickie!" Patti cried, launching into her first speech with all the finesse of a cheerleader at the Old Vic. "Wherefore art thou, Dickie?"

But she wasn't about to find out wherefore Dickie was because just then a woman in a T-shirt and faded cutoffs came lurching down the aisle, glugging from a bottle of whiskey.

"Bravo, Patti!" the woman shouted. "Break a leg."

Dickie turned ashen.

"Normalynne," he gasped.

Good heavens. It was Dickie's ex-wife, Normalynne Butler!

Aside from the fact that she was roaring drunk, she hadn't changed much since high school. Same scrawny body. Same lank brown hair in the same ponytail. Eyes framed by the same unflattering harlequin glasses.

Back then, Normalynne had been the kind of mousy kid who faded into the scenery. But she was far from mousy now.

"On second thought," she called up to Patti, "why don't you make everybody happy and break your neck, you conniving bitch?"

Then she turned to Dickie, who looked like he'd sell his soul to sink into a gopher hole.

"Can't you see, Dickie? She'll only make you miserable!"

"Somebody get her out of here!" Patti shrieked.

At which point, Conrad Devane and Kyle Potter rushed to Normalynne's side and began hustling her off the grounds.

"She stole my husband!" Normalynne wailed as they dragged her toward the house.

"Oh, get real, Normalynne!" Patti shouted after her. "Sooner or later Dickie was bound to leave you!"

The wedding guests, whose tongues were getting quite a workout that afternoon, were now yakking full blast about the latest development in this drama-fest of a wedding.

"Will you all please shut up?" Patti screeched, ever the gracious hostess.

Silence was finally restored and the show began. This time, with Shakespeare no doubt gagging in the great hereafter, Patti and Dickie managed to say their lines. They agreed to get married right then and there and avoid the whole icky double suicide mess.

But when Patti leaned over the balcony to blow Dickie a kiss, something happened that was definitely not in the script. A grating whine filled the air, and suddenly the imported Veronese railing gave way. A look of utter confusion crossed Patti's face as it came crashing to the ground.

She struggled to maintain her balance, teetering on the edge of the balcony for a few nail-biting seconds. But then, to the horror of everyone present, she fell, her wedding gown billowing out behind her like a tulle parachute.

The crowd gasped as she landed with a sickening thud on the marble statue of Cupid. According to the coroner, she was killed instantly, impaled in the heart by Cupid's arrow.

Poor Patti. Killed by the cherub of love. Not exactly the happy ending she'd been hoping for.

Of course, none of us knew about the coroner's report at the time. All we knew was that the bride, skewered by Cupid's arrow, was dead.

"She's not breathing," Dickie moaned over and over as he stroked her lifeless body.

Daphna Devane stood nearby, her face a frozen mask, while Conrad turned to his guests.

"I think you'd all better leave now," he said, his voice choked with tears.

In somber silence we filed across the lawn and then in through the house to retrieve our cars from the valets out front. As I inched along at the tail end of the line, I thought about Patti's fatal plunge. There was something about the way the railing had given way so easily, as if it had been barely bolted in, that roused my suspicions. Given Patti's endless enemy list, I couldn't help wondering if her death might not have been an accident.

At last I reach the foyer where my thoughts were interrupted by the sight of my wedding present on the gift table. I had a sudden urge to reach out and take back my $90 corkscrew. Yes, it was incredibly tacky of me, what with Patti lying dead out back, but lest you forget, I still hadn't been paid and my bank balance was pretty close to flatlining, too. I really needed that ninety bucks.

So I decided to go for it.

I hung back until everyone had filed outside, and when the coast was clear, I sidled over to the gift table. But just as I was snatching my gift, I looked up and saw Eleanor Potter coming down the Devanes' winding staircase.

I froze, caught in the act of giftnabbing.

I only hoped she wouldn't blab about this to Patti's parents.

But then I noticed something strange. I wasn't the only one who was embarrassed. The mother of the groom looked pretty darned uncomfortable herself.

Now, I knew why I was feeling guilty. The question was: what had Eleanor been up to?

"What a tragedy about poor Patti," she tsked. "We're all devastated."

Oh, yeah? She didn't look all that devastated to me. I remembered her vow to put a stop to the wedding. Killing the bride was one surefire way of doing it.

"I was just upstairs powdering my nose," she said with a stiff smile. "Now if you'll excuse me, I must go and console Daphna."

Her eyes drifted to the purloined wedding gift in my hand.

"Go ahead," she said, her smile growing conspiratorial. "Take it back. Poor Patti can't use it now."

She left me to rejoin the members of the immediate family at the back of the house, and I headed outside with my corkscrew. After giving my parking ticket to the valet, I hovered near some shrubs, hoping no one would notice my booty. I'd already been the object of enough embarrassing chatter, thanks to the flaming toupee fiasco. But no one even glanced my way. They were all too busy whispering about Patti's fatal plunge.

Waiting for the valets to retrieve my car, I wondered what

Eleanor Potter had been doing upstairs. I wasn't buying that nose-powdering excuse. Not for a minute. Why go upstairs to use the bathroom when there were about a gazillion guest bathrooms downstairs?

I was in the midst of these musings when I heard a car horn honking. I looked up and saw the most god-awful purple Cadillac roaring up the circular driveway.

And I wasn't the only one staring at this automotive monstrosity.

Everyone else in the well-heeled crowd had turned to gape at it, too.

The car came to a screeching halt, and then—to my utter and complete mortification—out popped Rocky aka Miss Emily.

Still wearing his *Practice Makes Pervert* T-shirt.

Oh, Lord. Obviously Brad had never called him to tell him he was going to make it to the wedding after all.

"Jaine, sweetheart!" Rocky waved at me, smiling broadly, his store-bought choppers glinting in the afternoon sun. "Here I am! Your neurosurgeon fiancé, Francois."

Now it was me they were gaping at—me and the wedding gift I'd just taken back from a dead bride.

And as I stood there, burning with humiliation, I knew that somewhere in hell, Patti was chuckling.

YOU'VE GOT MAIL

To: Jausten
From: Shoptillyoudrop
Subject: Getting Ready for Roberto

Marvelous news, darling. The Sunny Maintenance people
are coming to clean the carpets, which sorely need it. We
still have gravy stains under the dining room table from
last Thanksgiving! It wasn't easy getting them on such
short notice, but I begged and pleaded and they finally
agreed.

Not only that, I got the most divine curtains for the guest
bedroom, a lovely sage green which will work so well with
the new sage comforter set I ordered from the shopping
channel. What a bargain that was! Only $49.95—plus free
shipping and handling! It was so lovely, I ordered one for
you, too, dear. They were all out of sage, so I got you
Tequila Sunrise. It's an orangey-magenta color, a tad on
the loud side, but you can always tone it down with throw
pillows.

I've decided to welcome Roberto on his first night with a
genuine Italian meal. Edna Lindstrom next door gave me
the most yummy recipe for eggplant parmagiana. I cooked
a test batch and it was fabulous. Edna says the recipe
comes from the best Italian restaurant in Oslo.

And the best news of all—Daddy seems to have forgotten
all about Roberto. Apparently he had an argument with the
Tampa Vistas librarian about an overdue book, and that's
all he seems to be talking about lately. You know Daddy.
He always has to be mad about something. I'm just glad
it's not Roberto!

Oops. There's the doorbell. It must be the carpet cleaners.

Ciao, sweetheart!

XXX

Mom

To: Jausten
From: DaddyO
Subject: Civil Rights Violation

Dearest Lambchop—

Your mom's running around like Martha Stewart on speed, getting the house ready for her sleazy Italian lover. She thinks I've forgotten about him but I haven't.

True, I've been somewhat preoccupied over another matter. You'll never believe what happened when I went to the Tampa Vistas library the other day.

Lydia Pinkus, the insufferable woman who runs the place, claimed the book I was returning was overdue. A blatant lie. The return date was the eighth; anyone with working eyeballs could see that. But that self-righteous battle-ax insisted it was a "three" on the date stamp, not an "eight." Of course, if the cheapskates on the Tampa Vistas board of directors would invest in a new date stamp or get a computer like the rest of the world, we wouldn't be having this problem.

I stood up for my rights, as any red-blooded American would do, and refused to pay the fine. True, it was only 18 cents, but it was the principal of the thing! If nothing else, Lambchop, I am a man of principle.

And now I'm also a man without a library card. Because when I told that Pinkus woman I intended to keep my library book until she waived the fine, she ripped up my card.

Did you ever hear of anything so unjust? My civil rights have been sorely violated, and I intend to sue!
Lydia Pinkus will live to rue the day she ever crossed swords with Hank Austen.

I'm calling an attorney right now!

Your gravely wronged,

Daddy

To: Jausten
From: Shoptillyoudrop
Subject: Crisis Averted

Daddy's been on the phone all afternoon trying to get a lawyer to sue the Tampa Vistas library. He even called the immigration lawyer who advertises in Spanish on the back of the bus. Needless to say, nobody wanted to take the case, not over an 18-cent fine. Like they all told him, the Tampa Vistas library is privately owned. They can rip up anybody's card whenever they want. They all advised him to return the book and pay the silly fine.

Which is what he's going to have to do.

To think that he was going to sue Lydia Pinkus, an absolutely lovely woman and just about the smartest gal in the Tampa Vistas Book Club.

Well, at least that crisis is averted.

Much love from your frazzled,
Mom

To: Jausten
From: DaddyO
Subject: Change of Plan

Hi, honey—

Minor setback in my lawsuit. None of the attorneys I called met my specifications, so I've decided to take the case myself. I've always wanted to be an attorney, and now's my chance.

I can't wait sock it to Lydia Pinkus—right in her Dewey Decimal System.

Lots of love from,

Your daddy,

Hank Austen, Esq.

Chapter 11

Remind me never to read my e-mail on an empty stomach. I tootled over to my computer first thing the next morning and instantly regretted it when I saw the latest missives from my parents.

I shuddered at the thought of the Tequila Sunrise comforter set winging its way to me. My mom's heart is in the right place, and I'm touched that she cares so much about me. But we don't exactly have the same taste in, well, anything. Mom's idea of "a tad loud" is my idea of a raging inferno. I was certain the comforter's "orangey-magenta" color would be the soothing hue of neon traffic cones.

But the comforter set was a mere blip on my anxiety radar screen. It was Daddy who really had me worried. The thought of him running amok as an attorney—it was only a matter of time before some judge locked him up for contempt of court—was enough to ruin my appetite.

It stayed ruined for all of maybe thirteen seconds and then, as it so often does, came roaring back to life. I'm funny that way.

Minutes later, I was in the kitchen, slathering butter and strawberry jam on a freshly toasted cinnamon raisin bagel.

Prozac was at my feet inhaling her morning Mackerel Guts. I was still angry at her for masterminding Mamie's romp in the garbage. Now don't go shaking your head like that. She planned it, all right. I know she's only a cat, but you have no idea what she's capable of. Honestly, that cat could give lessons to Machiavelli.

I'd been giving her the cold shoulder ever since I got up, but it obviously hadn't affected her appetite. I guess she gets that from me.

Armed with my bagel and a steaming cup of coffee, I settled down at my dining room table and opened the morning paper.

Holy Toledo. Just when I thought I'd seen the last of Patti, there she was—plastered all over the front page of the *Los Angeles Times*. Above her Hermosa High yearbook photo, a headline screamed: *Socialite Bride Plunges to Her Death; Groom's Ex-Wife Brought in for Questioning.*

I read the story eagerly.

As I'd suspected, Patti's death was no accident. According to the police, it was murder. Someone had tampered with the balcony, loosening the bolts on the railing.

I gulped in dismay when I read that the cops had brought in Normalynne Butler for questioning. I could understand why they suspected her. Hadn't she urged Patti in front of scores of witnesses to break her neck?

But as you and I both know, Normalynne wasn't the only one who had it in for Patti. There was Eleanor Potter, Patti's future mother-in-law. And Cheryl Hogan, her ex–best friend. Both of them hated Patti's guts. And I was certain they were just the tip of the anti-Patti iceberg.

Besides, if Normalynne had been planning to kill Patti, why would she create a scene at the wedding, putting herself in the spotlight?

I thought back to the Normalynne I'd known in high school—a gawky kid, loping down the hall to her classes, smiling shyly when we passed each other. She never stood out—not until one fateful day in gym class. I remember that day—along with the day they started selling Dove Bars in the cafeteria—as one of the highlights of my high school years.

I'd always hated gym. I hated our thigh-baring uniforms and our frizz-inducing locker room. I especially hated our gym teacher, Mrs. Krautter, who, I was certain, had been a gestapo commando in a former life. Or perhaps even in this one.

Her routine never varied. After leading us in a sadistic session of calisthenics, she'd divide us into teams to play the sport du jour. She'd pick two team "captains" who'd then get to choose their teams. One by one, names would be called, the good athletes getting chosen up front, the klutzy ones at the end.

But no matter who the captains were, one person always got picked first. Patti. Not because she was such a good athlete. She wasn't. But the toadies wanted to curry favor with her. And the rest of us were simply afraid to cross her.

Just as Patti was always called first, there was one poor soul who was always chosen last: Linda Ruckle. Stocky and bow-legged, her round moon face dotted with acne, poor Linda was the object of Patti's merciless scorn.

Whenever she wound up on Patti's team, Patti would groan, *Oh, no! Not Ruckle!*, setting off a round a giggles from the Terrible Trinity. Linda would stare down at the floor, her face crimson with shame. And Mrs. Krautter never said a word. I don't know who I hated more at those moments: Patti or the teacher who should've known better.

Then one day, Mrs. Krautter picked Normalynne as one of the team captains. It was the first time I could remember her ever being chosen.

Normalynne loped out into the center of the gym. She and the other captain flipped a coin, and Normalynne won. She got to choose first. She pushed her glasses up on the bridge of her nose and peered around at the assembled cluster of girls.

"For my first player, I'd like to choose—"

With a toss of her ponytail, Patti got up from where she was sitting, assuming she would be top pick as usual.

But that day, Normalynne was about to make history.

"I'd like to choose Linda Ruckle," she finished in a loud clear voice.

Patti froze in her tracks.

"You've got to be kidding."

She stared at Normalynne through slitted eyes, the same look that had terrified all of us at one time or another.

A tense silence filled the air. Then Normalynne broke it.

"I choose Linda," she repeated, defiantly.

She knew there'd be hell to pay, that somehow Patti would get even—and damned if all these years later, she hadn't—but she went ahead and chose Linda anyway.

Now I've read about lots of courageous women in history. Joan of Arc, Mother Teresa, Donald Trump's ex-wives, to name just a few.

But in my book, they all pale in comparison to Normalynne, the girl who dared defy Patti Marshall.

Even more than her bravery, though, I was touched by her kindness. I'll never forget Linda's look of gratitude as she headed to the center of the room to stand with Normalynne.

Now, remembering Normalynne's kindness, I thought about calling her and offering to do some investigating on her behalf. Solving murders happens to be a hobby of mine— a dangerous hobby, I know, but one that sets my corpuscles racing. It's all very exhilarating, and—if you ask me—not nearly as terrifying as a bikini wax.

But for all I knew, Normalynne had a perfectly competent attorney who'd already hired a P.I. And for all I knew, Part 2, Normalynne really did sabotage that balcony. No, best not to get involved.

Instead, I started work on an assignment that had been phoned in the other day, a resume for a slacker whose biggest skill seemed to be napping on the job. It was a low-bucks gig, but low bucks were better than no bucks, so I set to work drumming up euphemisms for "college dropout."

But my thoughts kept drifting back to Normalynne. What if she needed me? What if she couldn't afford proper legal representation? Judging from the frayed cutoffs and drugstore flip-flops she'd worn to the wedding, I had a hunch she wasn't exactly rolling in dough. What if her attorney was some court-appointed dufus who didn't know a tort from a tart?

After a dozen false starts, I finally abandoned the resume and called information for Normalynne's number. All the operator had was an N. Butler in El Segundo. When I tried the number, a machine picked up, and a robotic voice instructed me to leave a message after the beep.

I left my name and phone number and offered my investigative services, then hung up, feeling a lot better.

Who knew if I'd reached the right N. Butler? And if I did, if I'd ever hear from her? But at least I'd offered to help.

My conscience clear, I breezed through the resume and faxed it off to my client, then spent the rest of the afternoon industriously vacuuming and paying bills.

Okay, so I spent the rest of the afternoon doing the crossword puzzle and soaking in the tub. I deserved it after putting up with Patti for so long.

Prozac, meanwhile, had been following me around all day, weaving in and out of my ankles, begging for love, as she so often does when she senses I'm miffed.

"Forget it, Pro," I finally told her. "I'm mad at you."

Moi? Enormous green eyes. *What did I do?*

"You know what you did. I don't know how exactly, but you instigated that whole garbage romp with Mamie."

More big eyes.

"Quit it, Pro. I'm not buying the Little Orphan Annie act."

I extricated her from my ankles and plopped down on the

sofa, where I started leafing through a pile of the catalogues that seem to grow like mushrooms in my mailbox.

Prozac came trotting after me.

Okay, okay. So I did it. We're better off without her, aren't we?

Then she leaped in my lap and offered me her belly.

Now that that's settled, how about you scratch my belly for the next four or five hours?

"There'll be no belly rubs for you, young lady. No way. No how. It's never gonna happen. So just forget it."

Okay, so I caved and gave her the belly rub. Pathetic, aren't I?

It wasn't until later that night when we were in bed together watching *All About Eve* that the phone rang and a timid voice came on the line.

"Is this Jaine Austen?"

"Yes."

"The same Jaine Austen who fell in Principal Seawright's lap at the prom?"

Would I never live that down?

"Yes," I sighed.

"It's me. Normalynne. Oh, Jaine," she wailed. "I'm in trouble."

Tell me something I didn't already know.

I drove down to Normalynne's apartment in El Segundo, a working-class town near the L.A. airport.

Her building was a sad stucco affair called the Casa Segundo. Although it was two in the afternoon when I got there, Normalynne came to the door in a pair of faded flannel pajamas, her eyes still crusted with sleep.

"Jaine, it's so nice of you to offer to help," she said, ushering me inside. Her hair hung in a limp ponytail, bangs flopping in her eyes. "Forgive the way I look; I haven't had the energy to get dressed."

She led me to a living room nicely furnished in beachy rattans, clearly put together in more energetic times. A jelly donut sat abandoned on a nearby end table. Amazing, isn't it, how some people can walk away from a jelly donut?

"Have a seat," Normalynne said, gesturing to one of two matching rattan armchairs.

She flung herself into the other, her long legs draped over one of the arms.

"Can I get you something? Coffee? Tea?"

"No, thanks," I said, wishing I could trot over and grab the donut. "I'm good."

And then out of nowhere an earsplitting roar filled the air. The furniture shook; the windows rattled. I was ready to dive for cover, convinced that El Segundo was under enemy attack, wondering if I had time to scarf down one last jelly donut before I was blown to smithereens.

"Don't mind the noise," Normalynne said. "It's just a plane taking off from LAX."

Omigod. If I had to live with that racket I'd be on round-the-clock tranquilizers.

"It used to bother me at first, but I'm used to it now. This was the only place I could afford after Dickie and I split up. Besides, I didn't want to stay in Hermosa. Too many memories.

"So," she said, forcing a weak smile, "how have you been?"

"Fine. And you?"

Talk about your inane questions. How the heck did I think she was? Surely her life wasn't an episode of *Happy Days*. She was a murder suspect, for crying out loud.

"Actually, I got laid off from work today."

"Oh, I'm so sorry."

"Me, too," she said with a hollow laugh.

"What sort of work do you do?"

"I teach biology at Crestwood."

I'd heard of Crestwood, a private school in Santa Monica, catering to the offspring of obscenely wealthy westsiders.

"Correction," she sighed. "I *taught* biology. I guess they didn't want a murder suspect mingling with the students. They pretended it was just a temporary leave of absence, but I doubt I'll ever be dissecting a frog at Crestwood again. Oh, what does it matter? I'm probably going to jail anyway."

"Normalynne, just because the police brought you in for questioning doesn't mean they're going to arrest you."

"I know they think I did it," she said, hugging her knees to her chest in a fetal position.

"What makes you so sure?"

"You saw the scene I made at the wedding. I still can't believe I got so drunk. I never drink. But I was so upset that day. All I could think about was that awful Hermosa High reunion when Patti first sunk her claws into Dickie.

"The funny thing is," she said, not sounding the least bit amused, "Dickie didn't even want to go. I had to drag him there. What a fool I was. We were having a good time, drinking punch and chatting with Veronica, when Patti showed up in a tight dress cut practically to her navel. She and Dickie locked eyeballs and that was the beginning of the end."

There was a catch in her voice, and for a minute I thought she might cry, but she held back her tears and went on with her story.

"I thought I'd gotten used to the idea of Dickie being with Patti, but come the day of the wedding, I went to pieces. I found a dusty bottle of whiskey in my kitchen cabinet and decided to add some to my coffee. Right away I felt better. So I had another cup. Then I skipped the coffee and started pouring myself straight shots. The next thing I knew I was barging down the aisle screaming at Patti."

"But I don't understand why the cops think you're the one who sabotaged the railing. Anyone could've done it."

"Apparently they've got a witness who swears he saw a woman out on the balcony the day before the wedding, tampering with the bolts."

"The day before the wedding?"

She nodded. "During the cocktail party."

"But you weren't even at the house that day."

"Yes," she sighed, "I was."

Ouch.

"I drove over to tell Patti off, only I didn't have the nerve. I sat in my car for more than an hour, trying to get up the courage to confront her. Finally, I turned around and drove home. Trouble is, one of the neighbors spotted my car parked out front. And now the police think I killed her."

I took a deep breath and asked, "Did you?"

"Of course not." Her eyes grew wide with dismay. "You believe me, don't you?"

"Yes."

And I did. I didn't care where her car was spotted; I simply didn't think she was capable of plotting a murder.

She sat back, relieved. "You know, I still can't get over you being a detective."

It wasn't the first time I'd heard that. Most people have a hard time buying a P.I. in a scrunchy and elastic waist jeans.

"I'm afraid I can't afford to pay you much." She shot me an apologetic smile. "In fact, I can't afford to pay you anything right now. Not without a job."

"Don't worry about it, Normalynne. If you get your job back, we can work out something then."

What can I say? I'm a sucker for a needy murder suspect. No wonder my bank balance is always so anemic.

After thanking me profusely for my help, Normalynne walked me to the door.

"Do you remember that day in gym class," she asked, a faraway look in her eyes, "the day I picked Linda Ruckle for my volleyball team?"

"Yes," I nodded, not telling her that was the reason I'd shown up at her apartment.

"That was a good day, wasn't it?"

"It sure was."

"I had a lot of good days back then," she sighed. "Oh, Jaine. How did it all go so bad?"

I left her with hollow assurances that there'd be lots more good days ahead, then headed out into the threadbare corridor outside her apartment.

Over the roar of a passing jet, I thought I heard her crying.

Chapter 12

Patti was laid to rest at the Westwood Mortuary, the crème de la crème of L.A. cemeteries, known around town as the final resting place of the stars. Rumor had it she was tucked away somewhere between Marilyn Monroe and Natalie Wood.

I'd read about the funeral in the paper and, suitably garbed in a black elastic waist pantsuit, showed up to check out the scene.

The same handsome minister who'd been set to officiate at Patti's wedding now conducted her memorial service in the mortuary chapel. Attendance was sparse, mostly acquaintances of Patti's parents. Interesting, I thought, after being so popular in high school, how few friends Patti had as an adult. The only one I recognized was Denise, decked out in designer black. I bet my bottom Pop-Tart there was no elastic waist under her suit jacket.

Not surprisingly, Cheryl Hogan was nowhere in sight.

With a blithe disregard for the truth, the minister blathered on about what a sweetheart Patti had been.

When he was through with his fairy tale, Dickie and Conrad took their turns at the mike and continued singing Patti's praises.

"I know Patti could seem a little demanding," Dickie began.

Yeah. Like Simon Legree at cotton-picking time.

"But underneath it all, she was a warm, caring person. A person I was privileged to know and love." His eyes filled with tears. "I cherished her with all my heart and will miss her always."

Conrad talked about how Patti was like a biological daughter to him, and how they'd forged a special relationship over the years.

Like Dickie, he seemed to speak from the heart.

Was it possible? I wondered. Had there been a likeable side to Patti I'd somehow missed? Or had she simply saved all her charm for the male half of the species?

When Conrad finished his tribute, Denise got up and took the mike. As she talked about how close she and Patti had been in high school, I couldn't help noticing that all her fond memories seemed to stop at graduation day. She spoke nothing of their friendship in recent years. Her words were loving, but her delivery was bloodless, like she was presenting a brief in court.

Once more, it occurred to me that Denise had grown estranged from her once-best friend.

The hunky minister returned to the podium.

"Would anyone else like to say something?"

He looked around hopefully, but nobody else was willing to put in a good word for the not-so-dearly departed.

Seeing he had no takers, the minister closed with a soulful reading of the 23rd psalm and then invited everyone to a funeral reception at the Devanes' estate.

Organ music swelled and the mourners began filing out of the chapel. Conrad and Daphna led the procession, Conrad holding Daphna by the elbow. But Daphna didn't seem to need any support. Her spine ramrod stiff, she stared straight ahead, as if daring anyone to feel sorry for her.

I sure hoped there were some actual emotions rattling around behind those glassy eyes.

Eleanor Potter trotted by, dry eyed and rosy cheeked. Was it my imagination or was there a spring in her step? Her husband walked at her side, his expression somber, eyes to the ground.

It wasn't until I started up the aisle that I saw a guy in a baseball cap glaring at me from the back row. At first I didn't recognize him, but then I realized it was Walter.

I nodded briefly and then hurried out to my Corolla before he could corner me.

The last thing I wanted was a tête-à-tête with Walter. Not after the way he'd been glaring at me.

No, sir. If looks could kill, I'd be sharing a crypt with Patti.

I debated about whether to show up at the après-funeral reception. On one hand, I needed to dig up some more facts on the case. On the other hand, I risked bumping into Walter. He obviously hadn't let bygones be bygones in the Flaming Toupee Affair. I had a hunch he'd be hanging on to that grudge for a good millennium or two.

Maybe I should just head home. But that was ridiculous. I couldn't let myself be intimidated by Walter Barnhardt, a guy whose claim to fame in high school had been blowing off his eyebrows in chem lab.

No, I'd go to the reception and poke around. If I ran into Walter, so be it. I'd offer my heartfelt apologies for setting fire to his hairpiece and be on my merry way.

My mind made up, I headed over to Casa Devane.

The house was shrouded in silence when I got there, a black wreath hanging from the front door.

What a difference from last week, when the grounds were festooned with perfume-enhanced roses, the air filled with strains of jaunty flute music.

No valets were lined up to take my car so I parked it out on the street, a shabby orphan among the neighboring Mercedes and BMWs.

As I headed up the driveway, the front door opened and Veronica stepped out. I have to confess I was surprised to see her, considering the big blowout she'd had with Patti over the missing frisee lettuce.

But it turned out she wasn't there to pay her respects; she was there to pick up a serving spoon she'd left behind.

"I forgot to take it with me," she explained after we'd exchanged hellos, "what with all the hoo-ha over Patti's death." She shook her head in wonder. "What a gruesomely ironic way to go. Impaled in the heart by Cupid's arrow."

"I can't believe the cops suspect Normalynne," I said.

"Really? I can. You saw the way she was carrying on at the wedding. She sure looked like she wanted to kill Patti. But then again," she added, laughing, "so did I.

"Oh, gosh." She checked her watch. "I've got to run. I'm late for a client meeting."

Drat. I wanted to question her and find out if she'd seen anyone sneak upstairs during the cocktail party.

"Any chance we can get together sometime?" I asked.

"Sure," she said, tossing me one of her business cards. "Call me."

And with that, she started off down the driveway.

"By the way," she called back over her shoulder, "they're serving deli. The roast beef is to die for."

I watched Veronica's retreating figure and wondered if she had been the one tampering with the balcony. It seemed hard to imagine she'd commit murder over a missing order of frisee lettuce, but one never knew, did one?

Ever see one of those wildlife documentaries where an innocent gazelle is minding her own business, chowing down on a blade of grass, totally unaware that there's a tiger crouched in a tree, eyeing her hungrily, poised to attack?

Well, that's sort of what happened when I stepped over the Devane threshold.

Bam! Out of nowhere, Walter pounced on me.

He claimed he was just leaving as I was coming in, that our bumping into each other was an accident, but it sure felt like an ambush to me.

"Walter!" I plastered a phony smile on my face. "How nice to see you."

He grunted, saying nothing. That glowering look he'd given me at the chapel was still operating on high beam.

"Well, it was sure nice running into you," I said, taking off for the living room.

"Wait a minute, Jaine."

Reluctantly I turned to face him.

"Yes?"

"I think you owe me an apology."

Okay. No biggie. I'd apologize, and that would be that. Over and done with. End of story.

"I'm so sorry about setting fire to your hairpiece, Walter. It was an accident, I swear."

I put on my most penitent expression—the same expression I use when I step on the scale at my doctor's office—and I was happy to see he seemed somewhat mollified.

"But if you want to know the truth," I added, "I think you looked better bald."

And just like that, he was glowering again.

"I am not bald!" he snapped. "I happen to have an extremely wide part."

Oh, rats. Just when he was about to forgive me, I'd dug myself deeper.

"You realize that you humiliated me in front of hundreds of people."

"I'm so sorry, Walter, really I am. I only wish there were some way I could make it up to you."

"As a matter of fact," he said, with a sly smile, "there is."

Phooey. I didn't like the sound of this.

"Oh? How?"

"You can go out with me."

"Go out with you?" I echoed, hoping I'd heard wrong. "*Out* as in *on a date*?"

"Yes. Unless, of course, you have another fiancé up your sleeve."

He was never going to let me forget that one.

"No, I'm not engaged. But I don't think a date would be a wise idea."

"Why not?" He thrust out his lower lip in a most unattractive pout.

"Because I'm not interested in you that way."

"Hey, I'm not asking you to marry me. It's just a plain old date. We'll keep it simple and meet for coffee. Get to know each other better. Is that so much to ask?"

Put that way, it didn't seem like much to ask. And besides, I could always use the time to pump him for information about the murder.

"Okay."

"Really?" His face lit up. "Oh, Jaine. That's great. Just great. It doesn't have to be coffee, you know. We can do dinner. I know a great discount sashimi bar."

I didn't even want to think what kind of glow-in-the-dark fish they served at a discount sashimi bar.

"Let's stick with coffee. And it'll be a platonic date. Just friends, okay?"

"Sure." Another sly smile. "If you want to start out as friends, that's fine with me."

I didn't like the sound of that, either.

"Call me and we'll set something up," I said. "I'm in the book."

Then I scooted off to the living room, feeling very much like a gazelle who'd just agreed to become lunchmeat.

I made a beeline for the roast beef which was, as advertised, to die for (as were the franks-in-a-blanket and potato puffs). After packing away enough cholesterol to clog the Alaska Pipeline, I got down to business and scoped out the room.

Animated knots of mourners stood swilling Chardonnay and chatting gaily. If they hadn't been dressed in black, I'd have sworn I was at a cocktail party.

Daphna and Conrad sat on a sofa near a massive stone fireplace, surrounded by a few friends who had the good manners to look suitably mournful. Daphna nodded woodenly at their words of comfort, while Conrad held her hand and did the talking for both of them.

As much as I would have liked to, there was no way I could question them about the murder, not now, so soon after the funeral.

I looked around for Denise, hoping maybe she'd have some information to impart, but she was nowhere in sight. I'd just have to chat it up with strangers.

Easier said than done. The Devanes' A-list friends made it patently clear to me that the only people they were interested in chatting with were other A-listers.

A typical conversation went something like this:

ME: *What a shame about Patti.*

GRIEFSTRICKEN MOURNER #1: Hmmm.

ME: *They say a witness saw someone suspicious out on the balcony.*

GM #2: Unnnh.

ME: *Tampering with the railing.*

GM #1: So, Paige, are you and Skyler going skiing in Vail this year?

Having struck out with the inner circle, I was about to call it quits when I spotted the Devanes' maid scurrying about, gathering soiled napkins and empty wineglasses. Maybe I could question her. She seemed nice enough the few times we'd crossed paths, and at least I knew she wasn't about to go skiing in Vail.

I quickly gathered some dirty plates and followed her down the hallway to the Devanes' extravagant kitchen—a culinary Taj Mahal complete with subzero refrigerators (yep, there were two of them), imported marble counters (no doubt mined from the same quarry as Michelangelo's *David*), and (this had to have been Patti's idea) a monogrammed doggie door for Mamie.

"Hi," I said, coming in with my dishes. "I thought you could use some help."

The maid, a sturdy woman with a copper complexion and cropped silver hair, looked up in surprise. I was happy to see she was alone.

"You shouldn't be here. Mr. and Mrs. D wouldn't approve."

"I won't breathe a word," I promised.

"You're Ms. Patti's writer, aren't you?" she asked, her eyes lighting with recognition.

"Yes," I nodded. "Here, let me help you."

And before she could stop me, I was loading dishes in the washer.

"You really shouldn't," she sighed. "But thank you. I could use the help. I told Ms. Daphna to get a caterer, but does she listen? Nooo. It's always, *Rosa can handle it.*"

"Well, one of these days, Rosa won't be around to handle things anymore. Me and my sister," she said, arranging wineglasses on a tray, "we're saving up for our dream house in Vegas, and then it's hasta la vista, baby. Ms. Daphna can find somebody else to be her slave."

Whoa. I'd struck a conversational gold mine. This gal was a regular Chatty Cathy.

We yakked for a bit about her Vegas dream house and then, as casually as I could, I said, "What a shame about Patti, huh?"

"Ay. What a terrible way to go. May she rest in peace."

Then she crossed herself and added, "Although the good Lord knows she never gave me any."

"I heard there's a witness who saw someone tampering with the balcony railing."

"Oh, yes. Julio," she said, now busy pouring wine into the glasses.

"Julio?"

"The gardener. I just happened to have my ear to the door when he was being questioned by the police. He said he saw a woman out on the balcony loosening the railing with a power tool."

"Did he see who the woman was?"

"No, it was getting dark and her face was in the shadows."

"I don't suppose he's around here now?" I asked, hoping I could sneak out and talk to him.

"No, he comes Mondays, Wednesdays, and Fridays."

The wineglasses filled, she picked up her tray. "I'd better get back in there now. These people don't eat much, but they sure can drink."

"Here, let me get the door for you."

"Thank you, *cara*," she said, as I held it open.

"No, thank *you*," I said, grateful for the dirt she'd so generously dished.

It looked like the gardener's mystery woman was the killer, all right.

I made a mental note to come back when Julio was working and pump him for more information.

Given my earlier chilly reception, I had no intention of returning to the reception. But, unable to resist the lure of the buffet table, I dashed back for one last frank-in-a-blanket. I had just popped it in my mouth when I overheard Eleanor talking to Dickie on a nearby settee.

"You know, honey," she was saying, patting his hand with tiny birdlike strokes, "sometimes things happen for the best."

He looked up at her sharply.

"What's that supposed to mean?"

"Sweetheart, I don't want to speak ill of the dead, but anyone can see that Patti wasn't right for you."

"Mom, don't start—"

There was an undeniable warning note in his voice, but Eleanor chose to ignore it.

"I'm just speaking the truth, Dickie. The biggest mistake you ever made was leaving Normalynne."

"Please, Mom. Not now."

"I don't know why you won't listen to me. Normalynne's such a sweet girl. So kind, so unpretentious, so—"

And then, like a long-dormant land mine, Dickie exploded.

"Shut up! Shut up! *Shut up!*"

All party chatter came to a screeching halt as Dickie reamed into Eleanor.

"You only liked Normalynne because you could walk all over her!"

"Lower your voice, please," Eleanor whispered. "People can hear you."

"I don't care who hears. It's over with me and Normalynne. I'm never going back to her." His eyes welled with tears. "Can't you understand? I loved Patti. I always will."

And then, as if waking from a dream, Daphna bolted up from where she'd been sitting on the sofa. She marched over to Eleanor, fire in her eyes. It was the first sign of life I'd seen in her all day.

"You never liked Patti, did you?"

Eleanor clamped her mouth into a grim line, saying nothing.

"Did you?" Daphna shrieked.

"No!" Eleanor snapped. "Of course I didn't like her. *You* didn't even like her. I saw how the two of you fought. My crazy son and your husband are the only two people on this planet who put up with Patti's nonsense.

"I don't care if she's dead, she was a dreadful girl. Rude. Insensitive. Nasty. Asking me to get rid of my mole for her wedding photos! The nerve!"

"I didn't blame her," Daphna cried. "Your mole is ugly. You're ugly. You're a joke."

"Look who's talking. Is there an inch of skin on your face that hasn't been lifted?"

Guests were following this exchange avidly, heads swiveling at whiplash speed. You can bet nobody was yapping about the ski slopes now. I myself was so engrossed, I could hardly finish my frank-in-a-blanket.

"C'mon, Eleanor," Kyle Potter said, hurrying to her side. "Time to go."

"Yes, go!" The veins in Daphna's neck throbbed. "Get out of my house."

But Eleanor wasn't about to leave.

"Not until I tell you what I think of you and your ridiculous Renaissance wedding. Patti couldn't get married to "Here Comes the Bride" like a normal human being. No, she had to have Romeo and Juliet and men in tights playing the flute! And those idiotic flaming punch drinks.

"No wonder she"—this said pointing to me—"set fire to the best man's hair!"

Oh, great. Now I was the center of attention. But just for a millisecond before all eyeballs were riveted back on the main event.

"You're giving me entertainment advice?" Daphna sneered. "You? The woman who caters her parties from the 99-Cent Store?"

"At least I didn't show up at my daughter's wedding dressed like a Vegas hooker!"

"Better a Vegas hooker than a menopausal frump!"

And so it went. A cat fight of the highest order.

And as the fur flew, all I could think was that in death as in life, Patti was still causing trouble.

Chapter 13

After the little scene I'd just witnessed, I couldn't help but wonder if Eleanor Potter was the killer. Clearly she'd hated Patti and was thrilled to be rid of her. But had she resorted to murder to spare her beloved son a ghastly marriage? I intended to find out.

The first thing I did when I got home—after feeding Prozac some roast beef I'd nabbed from the buffet table—was call Normalynne and get the Potters' address. I figured I'd drive down to Hermosa tomorrow and pay them a little visit. And while I was there, I'd stop in on another juicy suspect, Cheryl Hogan. She, too, had detested Patti. She'd told me as much in her drunken ramble at the rehearsal cocktail party.

I had no idea where Cheryl was living, so I spent the next hour phoning all the Hogans in the Hermosa area. I didn't find Cheryl, but I did find her parents. I told them I was an old friend of Cheryl's looking to get in touch. They seemed pathetically grateful to discover someone who actually wanted to talk to their daughter and eagerly gave me her number.

Cheryl answered her phone when I called, her voice slurry with booze. After I'd explained who I was for the umpteenth time, she agreed to see me when she got off work the next day.

I only hoped she was reasonably coherent when I got there.

I tootled off to bed early. Tomorrow would be a busy day and I wanted to get a good night's rest. I'd spend the morning trying to drum up some work and grab a quick lunch at my desk. Then I'd swing by The Cookerie to return that stupid $90 corkscrew and head on down to Hermosa.

I was curled up in bed, with Prozac blasting deli fumes in my face, when the phone rang.

"Hey, sweetie." Kandi's voice came on the line. "Want to grab an early lunch tomorrow at Century City?"

It was a tempting offer. I loved the outdoor food court at the Century City Mall with its sun-dappled tables and live music playing in the background. Plus they had some of the best hot dogs west of Coney Island.

But no. Absolutely not. I couldn't afford to take time out for lunch. Not with all the things I had to do. And the last thing I needed was a hot dog clinging to my thighs. No way was I going to say yes.

"Sure, Kandi. What time?"

One of these days I really had to work on my willpower. And I would. Right after I finished that hot dog.

"How can you eat that stuff?"

Kandi watched in horror as I scarfed down a hot dog smothered in mustard and sauerkraut.

"Don't you know the most ghastly animal parts go into those things? And they're positively packed with nitrates."

"Mmm, nitrates. Yummy," I said, taking a big bite.

"Really, Jaine. It's poison on a bun. How can you eat it?"

"Like this." I chomped down again.

"Oh, you're impossible!" she said, spearing a shard of broccoli from her chopped veggie salad.

We'd nabbed ourselves a prime table in the mall's outdoor food court. Kamikaze shoppers in their Nikes and Juicy Coutures rubbed elbows with office workers on their lunch breaks, and the warmth of the hazy L.A. sun felt good on my back.

"I've been meaning to ask you," Kandi said. "Did you ever find a guy to be your fiancé at that wedding?"

"Yeah, I got a guy from an escort service."

"How'd it work out?"

"Terrific—until one of the bridesmaids remembered seeing him at a male strip club."

"I told you you shouldn't have lied about having a fiancé," she said, with a smug smile. "You know my motto."

"*You're Never Too Young to Moisturize?*"

"No, silly. Honesty Is the Best Policy."

"Oh, puh-leese. This from the woman who's been lying about her age since kindergarten."

"Lying about your age doesn't count," she said with a dismissive wave. "Everyone does that." And then, deftly changing the subject: "So what about the rest of the wedding? How did that work out?"

"Not so hot for the bride. She got killed."

"Omigod!" Kandi sputtered. "What happened?"

"She fell from a balcony. Impaled in the heart by a statue of Cupid."

Her eyes widened.

"Wow. I read all about that in the paper. That was *your* wedding?"

"Mmmff." I nodded, my mouth full of nitrates.

"How come you didn't call me right away?"

I'll tell you why I didn't call her. Because I knew I'd be in for a bossy lecture (see hot dog lecture above) about minding my own business and staying out of danger.

"Don't even think about getting involved in this, Jaine."

What did I tell you?

"It's too late, isn't it?" she cried. "I can tell from that shifty look in your eye. You're already involved, aren't you?"

"Maybe just a little."

"Jaine, Jaine, Jaine. What am I going to do with you?"

"For starters, you can pass me the mustard."

"You can't keep running around chasing killers! Don't you realize how dangerous it is? One of these days I'm going to be reading your name from a toe tag at the city morgue."

"Until then, can I please have the mustard?"

She shoved the mustard across the table with an angry grunt.

"At least promise me you'll be careful."

I swore on her BlackBerry, which is practically her Bible, that I'd be careful, and we polished off our chow without any further lectures. (Well, I polished off mine; Kandi, as she always did, left a ladylike portion of salad on her plate.)

"Want to swing by Bloomie's with me," she asked, as we chucked our garbage in the trash, "while I pick up something to wear to Minnesota?"

"Minnesota? Why are you going to Minnesota?"

"To meet Carl."

"Who's Carl?"

"Didn't I tell you about him? The most wonderful guy I met on Air Date."

"Air Date?"

"It's the newest way to meet people online. You chat about where you're going, and then if you happen to be going to the same place, you book tickets on the same flight. Anyhow, it turned out Carl was flying to St. Paul to visit his folks, so I told him I had to fly there on business."

"Wait a minute. You're pretending to have a business meeting in St. Paul to hook up with a guy you met on the Internet? What happened to Honesty Is the Best Policy?"

"What's dishonest about that? I *am* going to St. Paul on business. The business of finding myself a suitable life partner."

Talk about your verbal tap dancing. If the bottom ever

falls out of the cartoon biz, Kandi can always get a gig as an HMO claims adjuster.

"So what do you say? You coming to Bloomie's with me or not?"

"Not. The only thing I can afford at Bloomie's right now is their shopping bag."

I hugged her good-bye and started for the parking lot.

"Promise me you won't go chasing after murderers," she called after me.

"I promise I won't go chasing after murderers."

Not right then, anyway.

First I had that ninety-dollar corkscrew to return.

Knights of yore had about as much luck finding the Holy Grail as I had finding a parking spot in Beverly Hills that afternoon.

Ferragamo must have been having a fire sale, because all the municipal lots were packed. After circling endlessly looking for a spot on the street, I finally broke down and pulled into the lot behind The Cookerie. I gasped to see the parking rate was an exorbitant three dollars every fifteen minutes. I got out of my car with a sigh.

The parking attendant, a young Hispanic guy, eyed my Corolla appraisingly.

"You want to sell it?" he asked. "I've got two hundred. Cash."

That made about $150 more than I had.

"Sorry," I smiled. "Not interested."

I tossed him the keys and he zoomed off to park my rust-mobile in the alley, so as not to contaminate the Rolls and Mercedes in the lot.

I hurried in through The Cookerie's back entrance, making my way past jet-propelled blenders and museum-quality espresso machines.

The same snooty blonde who'd sold me the corkscrew was

manning the register, ringing up a sale. I saw to my dismay that her customer was buying a dozen long-stemmed brandy snifters, each one of which had to be individually wrapped.

Blondie was taking her time, chatting gaily with the customer, a stick-thin fashionista sporting tight jeans and fake boobs. The woman looked like she had a few hours to kill before it was time for her next celery stick and was clearly prepared to kill them jawing with Blondie.

"These are such fabulous glasses," Blondie cooed. "I just know you're going to love them."

"I saw them in *Architectural Digest*," Fashionista Gal replied.

"They were in the *New York Times* magazine section, too."

"Really?"

"Yes, I think I have a copy here somewhere. Would you like to see?"

"If it's not too much trouble."

Oh, for crying out loud, I wanted to scream. *Don't go traipsing after some stupid magazine. Finish wrapping the damn brandy snifters!*

But Blondie had abandoned the glasses and was now busy rummaging behind the counter.

I looked around for another clerk, but the only one I saw was busy with a customer over by the espresso machines.

"Here it is!" Blondie exclaimed. I stood there, grinding my teeth as she and Fashionista Gal oohed and aahed over the magazine.

"Is there someone else who could help me with a return?" I finally asked.

"I'm afraid not." Blondie shot me a wilting look. "You'll have to wait your turn." Then she turned back to Fashionista Gal and, still blathering about brandy snifters and the *New York Times*, painstakingly wrapped the rest of the glasses.

I could feel the minutes ticking away. And at three bucks every fifteen minutes, it wasn't a very pleasant feeling.

Finally, when the last glass had been wrapped and Fashionista Gal had sailed off with her brandy snifters, Blondie turned to me with ill-concealed disdain.

"May I help you?"

"I'd like a refund."

I reached down to whip out the corkscrew, but before I could even get it out of the shopping bag, she said, "No refunds without a receipt."

A receipt? I rummaged around in the shopping bag, but it wasn't there. Ditto for my purse.

"Gosh, I don't seem to have it with me."

"No refunds without a receipt," Blondie repeated with a put-upon sigh.

"Can't you credit my charge card?"

"Sorry," she said, without a trace of regret. "The only credit I can give you is a store credit."

Oh, great. What was I going to exchange a $90 corkscrew for in a joint like this? Two $45 potholders?

With great effort, I forced myself to smile.

"C'mon. You can break the rules just this once, can't you?"

Apparently not. Not from the blistering look she gave me.

"But surely you remember me. You rang up the sale. For a $90 corkscrew."

"Yes, I remember you," she said, as if she'd spent the past several sessions at her therapist's trying to forget. "You were buying a gift for the Devane/Potter wedding. The cheapest gift on the registry."

Okay, so she didn't say the part about the cheapest gift on the registry, but trust me, she was thinking it.

"You were at Patti Devane's wedding?"

I turned and saw that the espresso machine customer, an

aristocratic dame with a beaky nose and thick mane of sun-bleached hair, was staring at me.

"So was I," she said.

"Small world." I managed a weak smile.

She, however, was not smiling. On the contrary, she looked horrified.

"And you took back your gift? With poor Patti lying dead in the backyard?"

"I'm not surprised," Blondie murmured.

"Wait a minute," Espresso Dame said. "Aren't you the one who set fire to the best man's toupee?"

"You're kidding!" Blondie gasped.

"It was an accident!" I protested.

"And then her fiancé turned out to be a male stripper," Espresso Dame blabbed to Blondie.

They both shook their heads, wondering how a social clod such as I had managed to wander into their rarified midst.

I grabbed my shopping bag and slunk out of the store, just as Espresso Dame was saying, "And it turned out the stripper wasn't even her fiancé. He was a paid escort!"

I could hear their *tsk tsks* ringing in my ears all the way to Hermosa.

Chapter 14

It was a picture postcard day in Hermosa—the kind of day I dreamed up by the Chamber of Commerce—with clear blue skies, fluffy white clouds, and gentle breezes rustling the palm trees.

I'd debated about whether to phone first before showing up at Eleanor's. But in the end I decided not to. I wanted to catch her off guard.

Luckily she was home when I got there. I found her in the driveway of her modest Cape Cod house, bent over her Civic hatchback, humming happily to herself. She wore a nylon jog suit that revealed an impressive array of figure flaws (it seemed I didn't have the biggest tush in Southern California, after all), and as I headed up the driveway I saw she was about to unload some groceries.

"Hi, there," I said.

She spun around, startled.

I had indeed caught her off guard.

A quick peek into one of her shopping bags revealed a champagne bottle and a bag of Oreos. It looked like somebody was getting ready to party.

"I'm Jaine Austen," I smiled. "We met at the wedding."

"Of course. How could I forget? The woman who set fire to the best man's toupee."

Jeez. From the fuss everybody was making, you'd think no one had ever seen a hairpiece on fire before.

"Can I help you?" she asked.

Translation: *What the heck do you want?*

"Actually, I've just come from Normalynne's."

A lie, of course, but she didn't know that.

"Poor Normalynne," she clucked. "I heard the police brought her in for questioning. From what I read in the papers, they think she's responsible for Patti's death."

"Yes, and she's terribly worried. In fact, she asked me to stop by and talk to you."

"Really?" She squinted up at me, shielding her eyes from the sun. "I didn't know you were friendly with Normalynne."

"Oh, yes," I maintained, keeping up my lying streak. "We don't see each other often, but we've been close ever since high school."

"Is that so? I thought you were Patti's friend."

"Oh, no," I quickly assured her. "I was just a hired hand at the wedding. Patti and I were never close in high school."

That seemed to score some points with her; at last she graced me with a faint smile.

"Anyhow, Normalynne wants to know if she can count on your support if her case goes to trial."

"Of course she can. Normalynne didn't kill Patti. She wouldn't have the nerve," she said, looking very much like someone who had more than enough nerve to pull off a homicide.

"Any ideas about who might have done it?" I asked.

"None whatsoever."

Whatever smile had been hovering around her lips now bit the dust.

"Now if you'll excuse me, I really have to bring my groceries in the house, otherwise my ice cream's going to melt."

Ice cream, too, huh? How very festive. It really *was* party time at Casa Potter.

And with that, she picked up her bags and turned to go.

"Just one more thing," I said, embarking on yet another lie—this one a whopper. "I happened to be talking to the Devanes, and they told me that the day of the wedding all the upstairs bathrooms were locked. Apparently Daphna didn't want strangers snooping in her medicine cabinets."

I couldn't see Eleanor's face, but I thought I saw her shoulders tense.

"Fascinating," she snapped, and started for her front door.

"I only mention this," I called after her, "because when we ran into each other in the house after Patti was killed, you said you'd been upstairs to use the bathroom."

She stopped in her tracks and spun around to face me.

"Okay, so I didn't use the bathroom. I went upstairs that day to get something."

The murder weapon, perchance? A power drill you'd stashed away after sabotaging the balcony?

"Mind if I ask what it was?"

"Yes, in fact, I do. But I've got nothing to hide, so I'll tell you. I went up to Patti's room to get a cameo Dickie had given her as an engagement present. It belonged to my mother. From the first, I hated the thought of her having it, and I wanted it back. Patti never appreciated it. All she ever wanted was diamonds.

"It was tacky to take it back," she said, shooting me a look that could melt steel, "but, if I recall, I wasn't the only one taking things back that day."

Bingo. She got me, right in my $90 corkscrew.

"I suppose you're right," I said, blushing.

"Surely you don't think I had anything to do with Patti's death. That was a terrible tragedy. Just terrible."

I blinked in disbelief as she tried to look mournful. Did she not remember I was standing not two feet away from her during her *Top Ten Reasons Why I Hated Patti* rant at the funeral reception?

"It's no secret I didn't like her," she said, as if reading my thoughts. "And yes, I'm glad the marriage is off, but I didn't kill her. Really, Ms. Austen, if I were the one who'd tampered with the balcony, do you think I'd tell a room full of mourners how much I disliked her?"

She had a point. If she were indeed the murderer, why call attention to herself?

But I still wasn't a hundred percent convinced. For all I knew, she'd blurted out her true feelings in a moment of uncensored madness.

I thanked her for her time and made my way back to my Corolla.

I was just about to take off when I saw a blue sedan pulling into the Potters' driveway. I watched as Kyle Potter got out of the car, briefcase in hand. He stood there for a minute, alone in the driveway, staring out into space, and in the bright afternoon sun, I could see worry lines etched deep in his face.

From the day I first saw him, he'd seemed concerned about Eleanor. Always trying to either hush her up or pacify her. I remembered the look of horror on his face at the funeral reception when she had her little outburst.

I wondered what was troubling him now, on this picture-perfect California day. Was it taxes? Business? The price of oil?

Or was he afraid that his loving wife, the woman who'd borne his son and cooked his meals, had sent their future daughter-in-law hurtling to her death?

Cheryl lived on the fringes of Hermosa, far from the palm trees and sandy beaches of the shoreline. Her apartment building was a dismal three-story affair, the kind of place with rusted hibachis and dying plants on the balconies.

It didn't surprise me in the slightest to see a VACANCY sign out front.

She came to the door in sweats, her hair a frizzy nimbus around her once-beautiful face. In her hand, she clutched a can of beer.

"C'mon in," she said, ushering me into a living room full of bland oatmeal-flecked furniture. I figured the stuff was either salvaged from a thrift shop or castoffs from her parents.

As I gazed at her in her stained sweatsuit, her bare feet cracked and dirty, once again I marveled at how far she'd fallen since her golden days in high school.

She picked up a bag of pretzels from the coffee table.

"I was just about to eat dinner," she said, ripping it open. "Want some?"

"Sure," I said, grabbing a handful.

I wish I could pretend to be appalled at her lack of couth, but who am I kidding? I've been known to dine on Pringles and martini olives myself.

"Let's eat outside," she said. "It's so depressing in here."

Minutes later, we were sitting out on her narrow balcony in sagging lawn chairs, beers in hand, the bag of pretzels on the floor between us.

"Nice view, huh?" she said. "More than ninety-nine billion sold."

"At least you're never far from a Quarter Pounder."

"I'm still not sure what you wanted to talk to me about." She propped her bare feet on the railing. Her toenails, I saw, were painted a bilious purple. "I'm sorry I was a little groggy on the phone last night, but I was sleeping when you called."

Yeah, right. Sleeping with her good buddy Mr. Budweiser.

"Have you been following the story of Patti's murder in

the news?" I asked. Somehow she didn't seem like the kind of gal who was up on current events.

"Yes, I saw it. The cops think Normalynne did it."

"Well, I don't, and I'm investigating the case on her behalf."

"Investigating? You mean, like a private eye?" Her blue eyes widened in surprise. "But I thought you were a writer."

"And a part-time private eye."

"Wow." She looked at me with unabashed admiration. "You've got two gigs going, and I can barely hold on to my crummy telemarketing job. You wouldn't believe how rude some people are. I've been cursed out in more languages than I knew existed. Oh, well. At least now I know how to say 'drop dead' in Hindustani."

Between the recently fired Normalynne and the minimum-wage Cheryl, I was beginning to feel like Hermosa High's Girl Most Likely to Succeed.

"So you really think Normalynne is innocent?" she asked. "I mean, you saw how crazy she was at the wedding."

"I also saw how crazy *you* were at the cocktail party."

"Hey, wait a minute," she said, sitting up straight. "I hated Patti, but I didn't kill her."

At that moment, I tended to believe her. I remembered how smashed she'd been at the cocktail party. It didn't seem likely she could've operated a power drill without hacking off a finger or two. But who knew? Maybe she snuck upstairs and did the dirty deed while she was still relatively sober. Maybe that's why she'd been drinking—to anesthetize herself to what she'd just done.

"You didn't by any chance happen to see anybody sneak upstairs that night?"

"Nah. I was too blotto to see much of anything."

"So you have no idea who might have tampered with the balcony?"

"Not a clue."

"Can you think of anyone who might have wanted to see Patti dead?"

"Take a number. To know Patti was to loathe her," she said, slugging down some more beer. "Lord, she made my life miserable."

"Even back in high school?"

"Especially in high school."

"But I don't get it. I thought you two were best friends."

"Back in the beginning, yes. I thought I was the luckiest girl in the world when I first moved to Hermosa and Patti took me under her wing. I'd never been very popular before, but when she swept me into her inner circle, everything changed. Suddenly everyone was nice to me. But it didn't take long to see how awful Patti could be. The same way she terrorized the rest of you, she terrorized me. Denise was strong and Patti respected that, but Patti sensed I was weak. And if Patti sensed weakness, she went for the jugular."

"Why did you stick around?"

"Every time I'd think about breaking things off, she'd start acting nice and lure me back in again. And it was high school. There was a part of me that was willing to put up with anything, I guess, just to be popular."

She sucked her beer for another comforting guzzle.

"So I hung in there. It was horrible. Patti got us to do things we would've never done on our own. We cheated on tests, drove without licenses—we even shoplifted at the mall. I was always terrified that someday we'd get caught. And then one day, it happened. A security guard caught us leaving the Gap with a sweater. Patti was the one who'd taken it, but she convinced me to put it in my purse. She told me her parents would never buy her the BMW they'd promised her for graduation if they thought she'd stolen the sweater, and she begged me to take the rap for her. She swore that her parents would take care of me, that they were good friends with the judge, and that the case against me would be dropped.

"And like an idiot, I believed her. The case went to trial, and I wound up doing probation. I lost my scholarship to UCLA and my life has been in the toilet ever since."

So that's what Cheryl meant at the cocktail party when she said Patti had ruined her life.

"But I don't understand. After all that, why did you still continue to be her friend?"

"Why?" She laughed bitterly. "I'll tell you why. She was sending me a check each month. Thanks to her daddy's money, she could afford to keep me living in the lap of all this luxury."

With that, she put back her head and drained the last of her beer.

"I need another. Want one?"

I shook my head and watched as she disappeared into the gloom of the apartment.

Was Cheryl the killer? She'd undoubtedly hated Patti's guts—with a rage that had been festering ever since high school. And yet, if she'd been getting money from Patti each month, she'd be one of the few people with a motive to keep Patti alive.

I really had to talk to the Devanes' gardener and worm a description of the mystery woman from him.

In the meanwhile, I grabbed a handful of pretzels and watched the sun set over the Golden Arches.

Stuffed from all those pretzels, I went to bed that night without dinner. For a rash instant, I considered digging into a pint of Chunky Monkey I had sitting in the freezer, but I remained noble and had a cup of Orange Spice herbal tea instead. It was surprisingly delicious.

I really had to get in the habit of having herbal tea at night instead of high-calorie snacks. I bet I'd lose a ton of weight. I got out my calculator and began running the numbers. If I gave up just 200 calories a day, that would be 1,400 a week,

6,000 a month, and 72,800 calories a year! Nearly 73,000 calories! My God, the pounds would practically melt away.

I was lying there, lost in a reverie of the new size 4 me in a string bikini, bouncing walnuts off my rock-hard abs, my cellulite a distant memory, when the phone rang.

"Hey, Jaine."

Oh, crud. Walter Barnhardt.

"I was just calling to set up our date."

I cringed at the "D" word. I wished he'd stop calling it that.

"Want to meet for breakfast Wednesday?"

I breathed a sigh of relief. Breakfast sounded harmless enough. And Wednesday was two whole days away. I'd meet the guy, slug down some java, expiate my guilt for having set fire to his toupee, and then bye-bye, Walter.

We agreed to meet at one of the gazillion Starbucks in my neighborhood.

"Sure you wouldn't rather have a discount sashimi dinner?" he asked. "I've got a half-off coupon."

"No! No discount sashimi!"

I hung up before he got any other nauseating ideas and then trotted off to the bathroom to brush and floss.

Okay, so I didn't trot off to the bathroom. I trotted off to the kitchen, where I made a beeline for that Chunky Monkey.

Yes, I know I'd just made a vow to give up high-calorie snacks. But you didn't really think I was going to let a pint of Ben & Jerry's sit untouched in the freezer all night, did you?

YOU'VE GOT MAIL!

To: Jausten
From: Shoptillyoudrop
Subject: Driving Me Crazy!

Jaine, honey, your daddy has been driving me crazy. Ever since he decided to act as his own attorney, he's been running around the condo, shouting, "I object!" and "I rest my case!"

When I asked him what happened to the package of Fig Newtons I bought yesterday, he refused to answer "on the grounds it might incriminate him." The house is littered with legal pads and *Law for Dummies* handbooks. He even bought himself a T-shirt that says, *If At First You Don't Succeed, Sue, Sue Again.*

He says he can't help me hang the new curtains in the guest bedroom because he's busy preparing his case, but right now all he's doing is watching old episodes of *Perry Mason.*

Meanwhile, he's the laughingstock of Tampa Vistas. Lydia Pinkus told her best friend Gloria DiNardo what happened, and of course telling Gloria anything is practically like broadcasting it on CNN. Now everyone is buzzing about how Daddy is holding a library book hostage over a silly 18-cent fine. I'll never be able to hold my head up in the clubhouse again.

Oh, dear. Someone's ringing the doorbell. I'd better get it.

XOXO,

Mom

To: Jausten
From: DaddyO
Subject: The Nerve of Some People!

You'll never guess who had the nerve to show up on our doorstep just now. Lydia Pinkus. The crazy battle-ax was raging and screaming at the top of her lungs, demanding that I return her stupid library book.

I calmly informed her that hell would freeze over first, and that if she didn't quit the premises I'd take out a restraining order against her. In my quiet but assertive way, I think I showed her just how formidable an opponent I can be.

Love and kisses from,

H. Austen, Esq.

To: Jausten
From: Shoptillyoudrop
Subject: So Darn Mad!

Oh, heavens. That was Lydia Pinkus at the door. She asked Daddy as nice as you please if she could have her library book back. He shouted at her to "quit the premises" immediately or he'd, and I'm quoting here, "ipso her facto!" And then he slammed the door in her face so hard I thought it would fall off the hinges.

I ran out after her with some fresh-baked brownies and tried to apologize, but before I could catch up with her, she drove away.

I'm so darn angry with Daddy right now, I feel trading him in for a new Toyota.

Your disgusted,

Mom

PS. I don't know why Daddy keeps referring to Lydia as a battle-ax. The woman weighs 90 pounds soaking wet.

To: Jausten
From: DaddyO
Subject: In a Snit

For some insane reason, your mother is in a snit, just because I asked that Pinkus woman to quit the premises. She practically threw my meatloaf at me at dinner.

Of all times for her to be mad at me—just when I need her to be my character witness in court! I had to soften her up somehow. So after dinner, I gave her a foot rub and agreed to pick up her old boyfriend at the airport.

What we lawyers have to do to win a case!

Love 'n hugs from,

H. Austen, Esq.

PS. I bet Perry Mason never had to pick up Della Street's old boyfriend at the airport.

Chapter 15

I woke up the next morning nursing a Chunky Monkey hangover.

After wiping sleep from my eyes—and chocolate from my pillowcase—I staggered to the kitchen where I tossed Prozac some Hearty Halibut Entrails and fixed myself a spartan breakfast of instant coffee and an Altoid.

With a much-need jolt of caffeine flowing through my veins, I hunkered down at my computer to check my e-mail. I groaned as read about My Father, The Budding Attorney and his ongoing feud with Lydia Pinkus. Leave it to Daddy to get into a battle royale over an eighteen-cent library fine. Poor Mom—the woman deserved combat pay. I was just grateful I was three thousand miles out of their orbit.

Not that things were so great at this end of the continent. Lest you forget, I still hadn't been paid for Patti's wedding gig, and my checkbook balance was teetering on life support.

So without wasting any more time, I printed out an invoice for *Services Rendered Mangling William Shakespeare* and tooled over in my Corolla to deliver it to the Devanes.

I was happy to hear the sweet sound of a lawn mower as I walked up their driveway. Which meant that Julio, the gardener, was out back somewhere. I fully intended to corner him and get the dirt on the mystery woman he'd seen on the balcony.

But first I had to drop off that invoice.

Part of me wanted to ring the bell and get a check in my hot little hands right then and there, but another part of me was embarrassed to be yakking about filthy lucre so soon after Patti's death. So I took the coward's way out and slipped the invoice in the Devanes' mail slot. If I didn't hear from them in a few days, I'd come back and talk to them in person.

Having dispensed with that awkward but necessary task, I trotted around back in search of Julio.

I should've known there'd be more than one gardener at a place as big as Casa Devane. At least four of them were hard at work, mowing, clipping, hedging, and pruning.

The grounds looked just as I'd seen them the day I first came to visit Patti. All traces of the wedding had been cleared away, except for the statue of Cupid beneath the balcony, which was blocked off—in a sad reminder of Patti's fatal plunge—by yellow police tape.

I made my way to the nearest gardener, who was busy trimming a magnificent lilac bush.

"Excuse me," I said. "I'd like to speak with Julio."

The gardener turned to face me. He was a tall, muscular guy in a baseball cap that said *Chuy's Landscaping*. Given that his work shirt had the name "Chuy" embroidered on the pocket, I figured I was talking to the boss man, Chuy of *Chuy's Landscaping*.

"Julio's not speaking with reporters," he said, waving me away like a pesky aphid. "Only the police."

Then he turned back to his lilacs.

"Oh, but I am the police!" I fibbed.

What's a little white lie in the pursuit of truth and justice?

I rummaged in my purse and fished out an old badge I'd bought at a flea market for occasions just such as this. The trick was to flash it fast, before anyone could read the words *USDA Meat Inspector*.

Happily, Chuy was content with a quick flash.

He nodded curtly and led me across the lawn to one of his workers pushing a lawn mower.

"Julio!"

The gardener looked up, startled, and Chuy motioned for him to shut off the machine.

"*Esta mujer es policia*," he said, gesturing to me.

Julio wiped the sweat from his brow and shot me a nervous smile. He was a frail man with darting eyes who seemed lost in the folds of his *Chuy's Landscaping* work shirt.

"Thanks," I said to Chuy, in my most authoritative voice. "I can take it from here."

He shot me a dubious look and then headed back to whack at the lilacs.

"Hi, Julio." I smiled encouragingly at the skinny gardener. "I have a few questions to ask about the woman you saw out on the balcony. I was hoping you could give me a better description of her."

"Sorry," he smiled apologetically. "My *Ingles* not so good."

"That's okay. I'll talk real slow. The lady on the balcony."

I pointed to the balcony.

"The one with the drill."

I pantomimed a power drill.

"*Sí,*" Julio nodded. "Lady on balcon."

"What did she look like?"

"I not see so good. *No mas sol*," he said. "No more sun. Was dark. *Oscuro*."

"Did she have long hair?" I asked, pointing to my hair. "Or short?"

"I not see good," he repeated. "*Oscuro*."

"What was she wearing? A dress? Slacks?"

Once again, I got an apologetic *oscuro*.

I tried to get a better description of the mystery woman, but all Julio was certain of was that he'd seen a woman and that he'd heard a drill.

Having finished with his lilac bush, Chuy now wandered over to rejoin us.

"Are you sure it wasn't a man up on the balcony?" I asked Julio. "*Un hombre?*"

"No," he shook his head. "No *hombre*. Was lady. *Mujer.*"

"Wait a minute," Chuy asked me, his brow furrowed in suspicion. "Don't you speak Spanish?"

"No, not exactly."

"The police know Julio's English stinks. They never send anybody who doesn't speak Spanish."

"Trust me," I said, determined to bluff my way through this. "I do this stuff all the time."

Experience has taught me that if you act confident enough, people believe whatever you say.

"Oh, yeah? Let me see that badge of yours again."

So much for experience as a teacher.

Looked like it was time to vamoose.

"Well, that about wraps up my questions. Thanks so much, Julio. Or should I say *Gracias*? Well, *buenas tardes, hasta la vista*, and all that."

With that, I gave them a ridiculously inappropriate military salute and hustled my gringa fanny out of there, my mystery woman as *oscuro* as ever.

My next stop was Denise Gilbert. Cheryl had hated Patti's guts; who's to say Denise hadn't been toting around her own hate-filled baggage all these years?

I got her business number from information and called her Century City law offices. I half expected her to turn down my call, but she came on the line with a friendly, "Hello, Jaine. How can I help you?"

When I told her I wanted to talk to her about Patti's death, she paused ever so slightly before saying, "Of course. I'm having lunch at my desk today, if you'd care to join me. I'll order us something from The Grill."

I have to confess I was surprised. The Grill is one of the premier expense account restaurants in L.A., famous for its hearty fare of steaks and chops. I'd pegged Denise as a dainty salad eater, the kind of gal who's stuffed after a few forkfuls of radicchio.

"Great," I said, and visions of T-bones danced in my head as I drove over to Century City.

Denise's office was on the zillionth floor of a towering high rise, a sleekly furnished affair with floor-to-ceiling windows and an IMAX-quality view of the ocean. On a clear day, she probably saw Hawaii.

She stood up to greet me, tall, cool, and elegant. Once again, I asked myself why a sophisticated woman like Denise had been hanging around a dingbat like Patti.

"Perfect timing," she said. "Lunch just came.'

She led me to a round glass table adorned with place settings straight out of *Elle Decor*, replete with silver, cloth napkins, and cut glass water goblets. Two covered dishes sat on ivory linen place mats.

What a change from my usual plastic forks and ketchup packets.

"Hope you enjoy it," she said as we took our seats.

Having had nothing since my Altoid for breakfast, I was salivating at the thought of something rare and juicy and smothered in onion rings. So you can imagine my disappointment when I lifted the cover on my dish and saw a pile of depressingly healthy greens.

"I ordered us ahi nicoise salads."

She ordered a *salad* from The Grill? With all those steaks and chops just begging to be broiled? The woman was nuts.

"How nice," I said, somehow managing to dredge up a smile.

I poked around and saw a few chunks of potato hiding in the greens. At least they looked interesting.

"So you wanted to talk about Patti's death." Denise speared a piece of near-raw tuna. "I still can't get over it. That awful fall from the balcony."

"The cops think Normalynne tampered with the railing."

"So I heard."

"But I don't believe it," I said.

"Really? After all, Patti did steal her husband. From what I heard, Dickie took one look at Patti at that reunion and fell for her like a ton of bricks. Normalynne must've loathed Patti."

"For a minute, let's just say Normalynne didn't do it. Can you remember seeing anybody else go up the stairs the night of the cocktail party?"

"Not that I recall, but I really wasn't paying attention."

"Well," I said, having polished off all the potato chunks in my salad, "I'm convinced someone else sabotaged that railing."

Perhaps you, Denise.

"I suppose you must really miss Patti," I said. "Being best friends and all."

"To tell the truth," she confessed, "we weren't all that close in recent years. I'm afraid we didn't have very much in common anymore. We got together every once in a while for old time's sake, but that was it. Actually I felt sorry for her."

"Sorry for Patti?" I blinked in surprise.

"She was one of those people who peaked in high school. After that everything was downhill. She went into business for herself a couple of times, but mostly she lived off the money she'd inherited from her father. I think at one point she was trying to sell a line of designer doggie clothes. But nothing ever seemed to click. It was all so pathetic. And then to have it end so tragically."

She shook her head and sighed. Why did I get the feeling there was something just a tad manufactured about her pity?

"Oh, dear," she said, looking down at my plate, "you've hardly touched your salad."

It's true. Alert the media. *Jaine Austen Leaves a Meal Unfinished!* I'd polished off the potatoes but couldn't bring myself to eat the raw tuna, and instead tried to bury it under the lettuce.

"I'm afraid you didn't enjoy it very much."

"Oh, no! It was delicious," I lied, wondering how long it would take to drive over to the nearest McDonald's for a Quarter Pounder.

"Well, if that's all you wanted to ask me, I really should get back to work."

"Of course. Thank you for your time. And if you remember seeing someone go up those stairs, give me a call."

I fished out a business card from my purse and handed it to her.

"Wait a minute," she said. "I just thought of someone. Dickie went upstairs that night."

"Dickie?"

The killer couldn't be Dickie. Julio was certain he saw a woman out on the balcony.

"Patti sent him upstairs to get her sweater. But he came right down again. I'm sure he didn't have time to tamper with the balcony."

"No, but he might remember seeing the person who did. Do you know where I can reach him?"

"Sure. I've got his contact information here somewhere." She went to her computer and clicked into her files. "Here it is. I'll print it out for you.

"You know, Jaine," she said, as the printer began whirring, "I owe you an apology."

"An apology? For what?"

"For being such a bitch in high school."

First Cheryl, and now Denise. It looked like Patti had been the only unrepentant member of the Terrible Trinity.

"I look back on how badly I behaved and I'm ashamed of myself. But I was pretty miserable myself."

"*You* were miserable?"

"My home life wasn't exactly *Ozzie and Harriet*. I guess I took out my unhappiness on others. I certainly hope I've changed since then."

She shot me a warm smile. At least, it seemed warm on the surface.

"Apology accepted?"

"Apology accepted."

She handed me Dickie's contact information.

"By the way, do you want me to ask Brendan if he noticed anyone sneaking up the stairs during the cocktail party?"

"Brendan?"

"The fellow I was with at the cocktail party."

Ah, yes. Mr. Rolex.

"Is he your significant other?"

"Nope. Don't have a significant other at the moment."

Grrrr. Here I'd gone through all that rigamarole to dredge up a bogus boyfriend, and it turned out that Cheryl and Denise were both just as single as I.

"Brendan is my campaign manager."

"Campaign manager?"

"I'm running for city council," she said, undraping a poster that had been propped up against the wall. A blow-up of Denise smiled out at me with the same warm smile she'd proffered with her mea culpa.

"If you're in my district, I hope I can count on your vote. Haha."

But she wasn't kidding. She really did want my vote. So that explained her heartfelt apology. Had she really changed, or was she just another pol on the campaign trail?

I thanked her again for her time and her salad, and headed for the elevator.

As I waited for it to show up, I remembered what Cheryl said, about how she and Patti and Denise had cheated and shoplifted their way through high school. If news of that ever leaked out, Denise's political career would be toast.

And I suddenly wondered: What if Patti had been blackmailing her old buddy all those years, threatening to blab about her checkered past?

Maybe Denise hadn't stayed in touch with Patti because she felt sorry for her. Maybe she stayed in touch out of fear of exposure. And maybe she got tired of running scared.

Sure seemed like a motive for murder to me.

Ten minutes later, I was in my car scarfing down a Quarter Pounder and fries, licking ketchup off my fingers with a sigh of contentment.

When I'd gobbled up my last fry and final pickle slice, I tooled over to Gelson's supermarket for a take-out lasagna. Now don't get your panties in an uproar. It wasn't for me. I was about to pay a condolence call to Dickie Potter, and I didn't want to show up empty handed.

The enticing aroma of lasagna wafted through the Corolla as I drove over to Dickie's house in Santa Monica. I came *thisclose* to plucking off a crusty corner of cheese and popping it my mouth, but you'll be happy to know I restrained myself.

Dickie's yellow VW was parked his driveway when I got there. He came to the door, bleary eyed, his hair tangled in messy clumps. Judging from the growth of stubble on his face, it looked like he hadn't shaved in days.

"Jaine!" He blinked in surprise. "What are you doing here?"

"Denise gave me your address, and I thought I'd drop by and check on how you were doing."

"Not so hot, as you can see," he said with a wry smile.

He stood there with the door half open, making no move to invite me in. It didn't take a rocket scientist to figure out he wasn't up for company, but I didn't care. I had to find out if he'd seen anybody going up those stairs.

"I brought you a lasagna," I said, holding it out, glad I'd taken the time to get it.

"Gosh, Jaine. That's awfully sweet of you." I made no move to go.

"Er . . . want to come in?" he asked, clearly hoping I'd say no.

"Maybe just for a minute."

And before he could change his mind, I scooted into his living room.

The place was very Tasteful Metrosexual, with lots of clean lines and recessed lighting. A large plasma TV was mounted on the wall, along with some gallery-chic artwork.

A far cry from the Dickie I'd known at Hermosa High, whose idea of high style was wearing two socks that matched.

"Have a seat," he said, "while I put the lasagna in the kitchen."

I eased down into a sleek leather chair. Across from me on a matching sofa, I saw indentations in the cushions where Dickie had been stretched out.

On an end table next to the sofa was a framed photo of Patti, taken in the gazebo I'd seen the day I first came to her house. The Secret Gazebo, Patti had called it when she pointed it out to me from the balcony. The scene of her many boffathons with Dickie. In the photo, Patti sat on the gazebo's white wooden bench, smiling seductively into the camera, unaware of the grisly fate that awaited her.

"I really should have offered you some of that lasagna," Dickie said, coming back into the room. "It looks delicious."

"Oh, no. I just had lunch. I'm not hungry. But why don't I cut a piece for you?"

"Okay, sure." He smiled wanly, sinking down onto the sofa. "I guess I forgot to eat today."

Unbelievable, huh? The last time I forgot to eat I was in my mother's womb.

I trotted off to the kitchen, where I found Dickie's stainless steel refrigerator plastered with pictures of him and Patti in various poses of premarital bliss: on the beach, at a barbeque, on the ski slopes, kissing under the mistletoe. Lots of Kodak moments, all oozing romance.

The lasagna was on the counter where Dickie had left it. Gad, it looked yummy, all tomato-ey and dripping with cheese. I cut him a big chunk and put the lid back on. Okay, so I didn't put the lid back on. I cut myself a tiny sliver, too. Okay, so it wasn't so tiny. Big deal. Like you've never had a Quarter Pounder with a lasagna chaser before.

I headed back out to the living room and handed him his plate.

"Here you go."

"On second thought," he said, staring down at it, "I guess I don't have much of an appetite."

Alas, mine was still very much alive and well, so I dug right into my slice.

"I'm so sorry about Patti," I said between bites.

"It's been horrible. Just horrible." He buried his head in his hands and groaned. "It's all my fault that Patti's dead."

"Dickie, that's crazy. How is Patti's death your fault?"

"If I hadn't proposed to her," he said, looking up at me with anguished eyes, "Normalynne would have never done what she did."

"You don't really think Normalynne is capable of murder, do you?"

"It's true she doesn't seem the type. But I never thought I'd be the type to leave my wife. And I did. I know it was a terrible thing to do to Normalynne, but I couldn't help myself.

That night I saw Patti at the reunion, it was like I'd been sleepwalking all my life, and I suddenly woke up."

I nodded in sympathy, but all I could think was that he'd have been better off asleep.

"I know Patti could seem difficult, but when you got to know her, she was a totally different person. So loving, and full of life. So passionate."

You know what this was all about, don't you? The "S" word. Sex. The Great Deceiver. Men are such idiots, *n'est-ce pas*? One frantic roll in the hay and they think Lucrezia Borgia is Florence Nightingale. Then two years later, they wake up and realize they're in the marriage from Hell and wonder how it all went wrong.

"I'll never meet anyone like her again," he sighed.

For his sake, I sincerely hoped not.

I polished off the last of my lasagna and got down to business.

"I don't believe Normalynne killed Patti, and I'm trying to find out who did."

"Who else would want to kill Patti?"

Far be it from me to break it to him that people had probably been standing on line for the privilege.

"That's what I'm here to find out. Denise Gilbert happened to mention that you went upstairs the night of the cocktail party. Do you remember seeing anyone on the stairs? In the upstairs hallway? Anyone at all?"

"Nope. Nobody."

"Did you see anything out on the balcony? Hear anything?"

"Not a thing. I've already been over all this with the police. I got Patti's sweater and went back down again. The only person I ran into was Veronica. She needed some help unloading champagne from her van. So after I gave Patti her sweater, I went outside and helped her. But that's it.

"Like I told the police, I wish I could be more help."

That made two of us.

* * *

It wasn't until later that night when I was curled in bed with a warm cat and a hot chocolate that I flashed on what Dickie said—that he'd bumped into Veronica on his way downstairs, and that she'd ask him to help her unload champagne from her van.

Why, I wondered, did she ask Dickie, when she had a staff of waiters at her command?

Maybe she hadn't really been looking for help. Maybe she'd been headed upstairs to loosen the bolts on the balcony. After all, Patti had threatened to ruin her business. And with Patti's A-list connections, surely she had the social chops to do it.

Just something to think about between chapters.

Chapter 16

Normally I am not a morning person (think Lizzie Borden with PMS), but for some reason I was feeling particularly peppy when I woke up the next morning. Indeed, I leaped out of bed with a smile on my lips and a spring in my step.

Then I remembered: today was my breakfast date with Walter Barnhardt.

And just like that, my spring sprang and my pep pooped.

It was with heavy heart indeed that I trudged to the kitchen and sloshed some Tasty Tuna Tidbits in a bowl for Prozac's breakfast.

Afterward I threw on my grungiest sweats, determined to be as unalluring as possible when I showed up for my date. I checked myself out in the mirror and was pleased to see that my sweatsuit bagged at the knees, sagged at the tush, and added inches to my waist. On the downside, though, my hair looked terrific. Just my luck, the weather was bone dry, so there was no sign of frizz anywhere, just a mass of soft, shiny curls. I corralled them into a sloppy ponytail and grabbed my car keys.

"See you later, Love Bunny," I called out to Prozac as I headed for the door. "Kiss kiss, hug hug."

She looked up from where she was clawing my sofa.

Whatever. Bring back food.

I drove over to Starbucks, giving myself a vigorous pep talk en route. How bad could it be? I'd have a cup of coffee with the guy, chat a bit, and then leave. I'd do penance for having set fire to his toupee and be a free woman again.

By the time I pulled into the Starbucks lot, I was feeling a lot better. Inside, the place was crowded, bustling with people getting their morning jolt of caffeine. I looked around for Walter, but there was no sign of him. For a giddy moment, I thought maybe he'd stood me up.

But no such luck. Because just then I heard:

"Hey, Jaine!"

I turned and saw him loping toward me with a supermarket shopping bag.

He, too, was wearing sweats, and the same baseball cap he'd worn to the funeral, still unwilling to expose his bare scalp to the general public.

After exchanging awkward hello's—mine was awkward; he was grinning from ear to ear—we headed over to the counter to get our coffees.

"My treat," he said.

"Absolutely not," I insisted, refusing to feel indebted to him in any way. "It's on me."

"Okey doke," he agreed, with whiplash speed.

We gave our coffee orders to the barista behind the counter, a stunning young man who no doubt was pouring lattes between auditions.

I checked out the pastry case and saw a chocolate chip muffin the size of a hubcap. I debated about ordering it. After the shameful way I'd gobbled down that lasagna yesterday, I knew I should be ordering something sensible like a bran muffin. But as always, Sensible Me lost the debate to Irresponsible Me.

"I'll have a chocolate chip muffin."

"No, she won't," Walter piped up. "I brought us breakfast," he said, pointing to his supermarket bag.

"I don't think they like you to bring your own food," I whispered.

"Oh, they don't mind."

Yes, they did. Our barista handed us our coffees, along with an exceedingly dirty look, and we went over to the supply table to add our milk. Walter reached into his shopping bag and whipped out a large Tupperware container. He opened it, and I saw that it was filled with Cheerios.

Then, to my utter mortification, he started pouring in Starbucks milk.

I turned to see if anybody was watching. Indeed, he had quite an audience. Several people were gawking at him, their eyes bugging in disbelief.

"You can't use Starbucks milk for your cereal," I hissed.

"I'm not using their milk. I'm using their half and half. Really, they don't mind. People do this all the time."

On what planet?

He poured out the last of the half and half from the urn, then shouted to the barrista, "Hey, fella. You're out of half and half."

Yikes. This guy had clearly been an honors student at Chutzpah U.

By now, word had spread among the patrons, and all eyes were riveted on us as we took a seat at a table by the window. If only I hadn't worn those butt-magnifying sweats.

"I brought two spoons," Walter said. "So we can share."

"No, thanks, Walter. I'm not hungry."

"Are you sure?" he asked, dumping three packets of Starbucks sugar onto the Cheerios. "It's dee-lish."

Never was I more certain of anything in my life.

"So," I said, trying to ignore the stares of my fellow patrons. "How's everything?"

"Pretty good." He dug into his Cheerios with gusto. "I ordered my new toupee. It's coming in from Taiwan any day now."

"Like I told you, Walter, I think you look fine without it."

"Wrong," he said with a dismissive wave of his spoon. "Women like a man with a full head of hair."

Hair, yes. Hamster fur, no.

I watched him shovel Cheerios into his mouth for a few unappetizing seconds, then sneaked a peek at my watch. Yuck. Only seven minutes had slogged by since I first walked through the door. I couldn't possibly leave yet. Oh, well. As long as I was trapped, I might as well question him about the murder.

"Sure is a tragedy about Patti."

"I dunno," he said. "If you ask me, Dickie's well out of it."

"Oh?"

"Patti would've made him miserable. I tried to warn him but he wouldn't listen."

As he shoveled down another spoonful of cereal, a crazy thought flitted through my brain. Had Walter sabotaged the balcony to spare his friend a miserable marriage? But that didn't make sense. Julio swore it was a woman he saw on the balcony.

"But Dickie stopped paying attention to what I said a long time ago. He's not the same person he was in high school. I think he only asked me to be his best man because we used to be so close." His eyes clouded over for a beat, but then he shrugged philosophically. "I guess that's what happens. People grow apart."

"Indeed, they do," I said, thinking of Patti, Cheryl, and Denise.

"Anyhow, I hate to say it, but the world's probably a better place without Patti. The only thing I'm upset about is that I wasted $29.95 on their wedding present. Plus ten bucks to have it specially gift wrapped."

"Twenty-nine ninety-five? I didn't see anything for $29.95 on their gift registry."

If I had, I would've bought it in a heartbeat.

"Oh, I didn't use their registry. The Sexometer came from a mail order catalogue. In fact, the same place where I got my toupee."

"The Sexometer?"

"It's like a kazoo with different buttons on it, so that your partner can read your sexual temperature. There's *On Fire, Warm, Tepid,* and *Honey I've Got a Headache*. What a great idea, huh?"

"Uh-huh." I nodded woodenly, aghast at this new low in bad taste.

"I wanted to take it back from the gift table so I could get a refund, but who does a tacky thing like that?"

A quick change of subject was definitely in order. So I asked Walter what I'd been asking everybody else, if he'd seen anyone sneak upstairs during the cocktail party. Like everybody else, he saw nada.

"If you remember," he said, "that night I only had eyes for you."

I remembered, all right. Only too well.

At last he'd finished his tub of cereal and slurped up every last drop of half and half. Enough time had elapsed, I thought, for me to make my exit. I was just about to fumpher an excuse and make a break for it when he cleared his throat and said:

"Say, Jaine. Have you heard about the Hermosa High reunion this weekend?"

"No, I guess I'm on their Do Not Call list."

"Last year's reunion was such a big success, they decided to have another one. Anyhow, I was wondering if you'd like to go with me."

No way. Never in a zillion years. Not if he were the last insurance actuary on the face of the earth.

"I'm afraid not, Walter."

His mouth opened in a tiny Cheerio of disappointment.

"Please don't feel bad," I said.

"Of course I feel bad. You know I've always had a crush on you, Jaine, ever since the day I first saw you eating M&M's in assembly. I must've invited you to my house a hundred times to see my ant farm, but you never came. And then, in senior year, you broke my heart."

"I broke your heart?"

"Remember how I asked you to the prom and you said you weren't going and then you showed up with Dylan Janovici?"

"Walter, you asked me to the prom on the first day of school. By June, I'd forgotten all about it."

"I stayed home that night and watched Lawrence Welk with my parents while you were out dancing with Dylan."

I thought back to that ghastly evening, being tossed around on the dance floor like a ship in a hurricane, and the utter humiliation of landing in Principal Seawright's lap.

"If it's any consolation," I said, "I had a horrible time, too."

"It couldn't have been worse than mine. That night was the unhappiest night of my life."

"I'm so sorry, Walter. I never meant to hurt you."

Ironic, isn't it? While Patti and Denise and Cheryl were torturing the rest of the student body, I'd been unwittingly torturing poor Walter. High school was undoubtedly a daisy chain of torture, a teenage caste system fueled by raging hormones and gross insecurities.

"That's okay," he sighed. "I got over it. And I'll get over this, too."

He sat there with a piece of Cheerio on his chin, and I was suddenly awash in a wave of pity. Walter wasn't such a bad fellow. Would it kill me to spend one more night with him?

And so, my heart overflowing with the milk of human kindness, I heard myself saying:

"I'll go to the reunion with you, Walter."

"You will?" His eyes lit up with gratitude.

"But not as a date. As friends."

"Yeah, yeah, whatever," he said, ignoring my caveat. "I promise you won't regret it!"

Of course I would.

In fact, I regretted it not thirty seconds later when he scooped up a plateful of free brownie samples from the counter and said to the barista, "Wrap these to go."

Yep, right then and there, my milk of human kindness began curdling.

Chapter 17

I waited in the Corolla until I saw Walter drive off, then scooted back to Starbucks to get what I'd been lusting after since I first saw it in the display case—that big, fat chocolate chip muffin.

"Sorry," the stunning barista smirked when I put in my order, "we're all out. But we've got a fresh plate of biscotti samples. Shall I wrap them to go?"

Harty bleeping har.

"I'll have a bran muffin, please," I said with all the dignity I could muster.

"Don't forget to help yourself to a cup of half and half. We just stocked up."

Quite the comedian, wasn't he?

I grabbed my muffin and polished it off in my car, safe from the barbs of the wise guy barista. Then, feeling somewhat revived, I set off to pay a little visit to Veronica. As much as I liked her, I had to consider her a suspect. Not only was she seen near the staircase the night of the cocktail party, but given the fact that Patti had threatened to ruin her business, she had a strong motive for wanting her out of the way.

Hubbard's Cupboard was a tiny storefront tucked away on Melrose Avenue among a string of trendy boutiques and hair salons.

Several customers were looking over menu books in the reception area when I came in, oohing and aahing over appetizers.

I made my way past them to a counter where I was greeted by a spiky-haired sprite with more earrings in her earlobes than I had in my entire jewelry box.

"Hi, there!" she chirped. "Welcome to Hubbard's Cupboard. Can we help you cater the party of your dreams?"

"No," I demurred, not mentioning that my usual caterer of choice was Colonel Sanders. "Actually, I'm here to see Veronica."

"Is she expecting you?"

Indeed she was. I'd called her on the way over and told her I needed to speak with her on a matter of utmost importance.

The sprite led me to an industrial kitchen in the rear of the store where I found Veronica in her chef's jacket, hard at work stuffing squabs.

"We're getting ready for a big party tonight," she said, her face flushed from the heat of the kitchen. "Hope you don't mind if I do some prep work while we talk."

"No, not at all."

I sat across from her at a huge kitchen island and watched as she proceeded to stuff the squabs, sticking her fingers up their privates like an assembly line gynecologist.

"So what's up?" she asked as she made her way down the row of birds.

I told her I was investigating Patti's murder.

She looked up in amazement.

You're a private eye?

I couldn't blame her for being surprised. Back in high school, I had a hard time finding my own locker.

"It's more of a hobby than a job."

"Sounds like a dangerous hobby."

"It can be," I said, trying to sound a lot tougher than the

marshmallow I was. "Anyhow," I proceeded, getting down to business, "I saw Dickie yesterday."

"Surely you don't suspect him? Dickie was devastated when Patti died."

"No, I don't suspect him. But he mentioned that he ran into you in the hallway the night of the cocktail party. He said you asked him for help unloading champagne from your van."

I looked for a reaction, a flicker of guilt. But she just went on stuffing her squabs, totally unfazed.

"I hated to bother him, but my waiters were all busy serving the guests. I was short-staffed that night. If you remember, darling Patti made me send one of my guys home because his hair clashed with her dress."

"Oh, right."

I'd forgotten all about that. It certainly explained why Veronica would've asked Dickie for help.

"Wait a minute," she said, the gist of my conversation beginning to sink in. "Why are you asking me about where *I* was that night? You don't think I had anything to do with the murder, do you?"

Standing there with a dish towel slung over her shoulder and a small dot of flour on the tip of her nose, she looked about as capable of murder as Betty Crocker. I was beginning to feel a tad foolish.

"Well," I fumphered, "Patti did threaten to ruin your business."

"Oh, please," she laughed. "If I took every threat I've ever received in this business seriously, I would've committed murder—or suicide—long ago. I've been chewed out by people far more important than Patti. And you know what? Six months later, they're calling me to cater another party."

Our tête-à-tête was interrupted just then by the ding of an oven timer.

"My empanadas!"

Veronica dashed over to one of the stainless steel ovens and took out a sheet of golden brown pastry pockets.

"It's a new recipe," she said, transferring them to a plate. "Chicken cheese. What do you think?"

She held them out for my inspection.

"They look fantastic."

"C'mon." She grinned, "let's do some taste testing."

Needless to say, I didn't have to be asked twice.

I bit into a divine mixture of flaky pastry dough, chicken, and melted cheese. My taste buds were doing the cha-cha.

And just like that, Veronica sank to the bottom of my suspect list. Anyone who cooked something this heavenly couldn't possibly be a killer, could she?

I assured her the empanadas were divine and thanked her for putting up with my prying questions.

"By the way," I said as I got up to leave, "I don't suppose you saw anyone heading up the stairs the night of the cocktail party?"

"As a matter of fact, I did. Eleanor Potter."

Eleanor Potter, huh? Now there was a suspect who just kept popping up over and over again.

Looked like it was time for another drive down to Hermosa.

"What now?" Eleanor snapped when she saw me on her doorstep.

Arms folded tightly across her ample chest, she glared at me in a most unfriendly manner. So palpable was her irritation, I was surprised she hadn't yanked the welcome mat out from under my feet.

"Well?" She tapped her foot impatiently. "What is it?"

There was no gentle way of approaching this; I was going to have to dive right in.

"Look, Eleanor. I've just been talking to Veronica the caterer."

"Oh? Are you and your 'fiancé' planning a wedding? Better take out plenty of fire insurance."

Boy, everybody was a comedian today.

"Veronica says she saw you sneaking upstairs the night of the cocktail party."

True, Veronica hadn't used the word *sneaking*. I just threw that in for dramatic effect.

"In case you weren't aware of it," I added, "that's when the police say the murderer tampered with the railing on the—"

But I never did get to "balcony," because by then she'd slammed the door in my face.

Okay, she was playing hardball. So would I.

"Either you talk to me," I shouted, "or I talk to the police."

A long beat, and then the door slowly opened.

My threat had worked. Eleanor stood there, her shoulders slumped in resignation, the starch knocked out of her.

"C'mon in," she sighed.

I followed her into what I can only describe as a shrine to Dickie Potter. Sure, there were the requisite sofa and chairs and coffee table. But what instantly caught my eye were the gazillion photos of Dickie scattered around the Potters' living room, from diaper days to graduation and beyond.

Framed over the fireplace was a wedding portrait of Dickie and Normalynne.

Patti must've loved that.

Eleanor waved me to an armchair and sunk down into a nubby plaid recliner, propping her Easy Spirits onto the footrest.

"I went upstairs," she said, "to look for sex tapes."

"Sex tapes?"

"I'd heard on the grapevine that Patti liked to tape her sexual encounters, that she'd been doing it ever since high school. I figured if I could find those tapes and show them to Dickie, he'd see what a slut she was and call off the wedding."

Not necessarily, I thought. Some men would have the tapes copied and transferred to DVD.

"I searched her bedroom, but all I found was some body chocolate and edible underwear."

She leaned back in the recliner and closed her eyes, as if weary from the effort of reliving it all.

"Go to the police if you want," she sighed, "but that's what really happened."

I was inclined to believe her. There was something about her story that rang true. A tad disappointing, I must admit. Just when I'd been certain I'd been zeroing in on the killer.

"Well, if that's all," she said, sitting up in the recliner, "I really should be fixing lunch."

But it wasn't all. Not by a long shot. Because just then Kyle Potter came wandering into the room, in jeans and a work shirt, a tool belt hanging from his waist.

"There you are, Eleanor. Have you seen my monkey wrench?"

Then he glanced over and saw me.

"Oh, hi, Jaine. What are you doing here?"

"Jaine thinks I'm the one who sabotaged Patti's balcony."

"She *what*?" His normally mild blue eyes clouded over with anger.

"Now, Eleanor," I protested, "that's not exactly what I said—"

"Someone saw me going upstairs the night of the cocktail party, and now Jaine's convinced I'm the one who killed Patti."

"Why did you even let her in the house?" he shouted at his wife. This was the first time I'd ever heard Kyle Potter raise his voice. Eleanor shrank back, afraid. And she wasn't the only one. I was feeling a bit skittish myself.

"She threatened to go to the police."

Kyle turned to me, his eyes blazing, a small vein throbbing in his temple.

"You do," he hissed, "and you'll live to regret it."

Trust me, I was regretting it already.

"Oh, heavens, no!" I started babbling. "I'm not going to the police. What a crazy idea that was, huh? Anyone can see you two are model citizens. Probably don't even have an outstanding parking ticket. And speaking of tickets, I'd better get going if I don't want to get one. Well, it's been swell chatting. Let's keep in touch!"

And with that impressive display of cowardice, I beat a hasty retreat to the safety of my Corolla.

I took off for the freeway, mulling over what I'd just witnessed. What an eye-opener that had been. There was a whole other Kyle Potter most people didn't see. An angry guy with an explosive temper. And how about that tool belt? Clearly he knew his way around a power drill.

I remembered standing next to the Potters at the rehearsal cocktail party and overhearing Eleanor bitch to Kyle about Patti. He'd told her not to worry, assuring her everything would be okay. At the time I thought he was just pacifying her. But now I wondered: Maybe he wasn't worried about Patti, *because he already knew she'd be dead.*

But Julio insisted the person he saw out on the balcony that night was a woman.

Was it possible Julio had been wrong? Was there any way he could have mistaken 6'3" Kyle Potter for a woman in the dusky sunset?

Not bloody likely.

I groaned in frustration. Another juicy suspect bites the dust.

*   *   *

Traffic was a nightmare. It doesn't take much for traffic to go crazy on the 405 Freeway. Somebody has a flat tire in Cleveland and traffic backs up on the 405. On this particular day, I believe it was backed up to Acapulco.

I was sitting in my car, watching the weeds grow on the shoulder of the freeway, when I realized that I was a quarter of a mile away from El Segundo, where Normalynne lived. I'd been meaning to check in on her and now was as good a time as any. At least it would get me out of this automotive hellhole.

A few eons later, I made it to the El Segundo exit and hit the off-ramp with all the exhilaration of an ex-con on his first day of freedom.

What a thrill to zoom along in street traffic at thirty miles an hour.

At last I arrived at Casa Segundo, just in time to see Normalynne coming out the front door of the building, dressed in a conservative skirt and blazer, sensible pumps on her feet. For a minute I thought she got her teaching job back.

But then I saw she was not alone. Two policemen were at her side.

"Normalynne!" I cried, racing to her. "What's going on?"

"Oh, Jaine!" Her eyes, magnified by her strong glasses, were wide with panic. "I'm going to jail."

"Oh, no," I moaned.

"And they won't let me take anything to read. I'll go crazy in jail without a book."

"I'm sure you can get a book from the prison library," said one of the cops, a brawny fireplug of a guy with a surprisingly gentle voice.

Far be it from me to break it to these people, but the lack of decent reading material in jail would be the least of Normalynne's problems.

"I don't understand. Why are they arresting you?"

"They found a power drill hidden in the bushes on the Devane estate."

"I don't get it. How does that implicate you?"

"Because they found the matching drill bit somewhere else."

"Where?" I asked, with a growing sense of foreboding.

"In the backseat of my car."

Chapter 18

Normalynne's arrest was all over the TV that night. Every station I turned to had footage of her being escorted to jail, blinking into the cameras like a myopic deer in the headlights. Her wispy court-appointed attorney, obviously not used to trying high-profile cases, looked almost as scared as Normalynne.

"No comment," he mumbled to the reporters, about as dynamic as a bowl of oatmeal.

Word of Patti's bridal tantrums had spread, and some of the more scurrilous news outlets were calling Normalynne *The Bridezilla Killer*. Ah, yes. That would go nicely on her resume.

I must confess that for a few minutes I wondered if Normalynne really *had* tampered with the balcony. After all, the police did find the drill bit in her car. But, no. My gut still told me she was innocent. Someone planted that drill bit there to incriminate her.

The question was—who?

I spent a restless night, hoping I'd wake up the next morning with some answers, but all I woke up with was a cat on my chest, clawing for her breakfast.

"This is so frustrating, Pro. Just when I'm convinced I've got a hot suspect, they start looking innocent."

She peered at me through slitted eyes.

And this is important to me because?

With a weary sigh, I hauled myself out of bed and slopped some Hearty Halibut Innards into her bowl. Then I threw on my sweats and grabbed my keys.

"I need to clear my brain," I told Prozac, who had finished inhaling her breakfast and was now stretched out on my computer keyboard. "I'm going for a jog."

Oh, please. What jog? We both know you're going for jelly donuts.

Shows you how much she knew. I did not go for jelly donuts. I went for *chocolate glazed* donuts.

Which wasn't as decadent as it sounds. Chocolate is a known stimulant, and I was hoping a healthy dose of the stuff would get my brain cells hopping. Unfortunately the only thing that got stimulated were the fat cells picnicking on my thighs.

Back home, I found Prozac napping on my keyboard where I'd left her.

"My, that jog was refreshing!" I exclaimed.

She opened one eye and shot me a piercing look.

Oh, please. I can smell the chocolate on your breath from here.

By now, the mailman had come and an avalanche of envelopes were scattered across the floor. I gathered them up and saw to my dismay that most of them were bills. Big fat ones. Several accompanied by sweet notes informing me that if they weren't paid soon, I'd be hearing from my friendly neighborhood collection agency.

There was no getting around it. I simply had to stop by the Devanes and ask them for the three thousand dollars they owed me. I hadn't heard a word from them since I left my invoice in their mail slot, and I couldn't let it go any longer.

And while I was at it, I absolutely had to get my money back on that corkscrew. I'd be damned if I let ninety dollars sail down the drain.

I spent the next several hours scouring my apartment for the missing receipt. After searching through every possible receptacle (including Prozac's litter basket), I finally found it where it was all along—in my purse! Stuck to an old Almond Joy. I could've kicked myself for not seeing it when I was at The Cookerie, but that snooty blond salesclerk had me flustered.

Oh, well. This time, I'd show her who was boss.

The Cookerie was having a sale when I showed up, having reduced their prices from obscenely expensive to merely ridiculously expensive. And the customers were out in droves, lined up in their Manolos, eager to part with their money. There's nothing rich Angelenos like better than status symbols on sale.

I was hoping maybe Blondie wouldn't be there, but no such luck. There she was, glued behind the counter, as usual.

The good news was, she wasn't alone. A sweet young thing with a friendly smile was at her side ringing up sales.

I took my place at the end of the line, praying that I'd get the Sweet Young Thing. And it looked like I was going to get my wish. When I got to the front of the line, Blondie was busy wrapping a bunch of glasses—and we all know how long *that* can take. The Sweet Young Thing, I was delighted to see, was just finishing up with a customer, a nipped and tucked brunette whose face was as tight as a snare drum.

"Here you go," the SYT said, handing the brunette a Cookerie shopping bag. "I hope you enjoy your waffle iron."

"Oh, I know I will," the brunette replied, taking the bag.

Her sale complete, the SYT looked up at me.

"Next, please," she said with a friendly smile

And I was just about to step up to the counter, when the waffle iron lady sauntered back.

"On second thought," she said, "I think I'll take another one of these for my daughter."

Wait a minute! Why didn't she think of this twenty minutes ago, when she was shopping? Why the heck did her daughter need a waffle iron, anyway, when she could just pop an Eggo in the toaster? And who was she kidding? The last time this bag of bones had eaten a waffle, she'd been in kindergarten.

Make her go to the back of the line! I wanted to shout.

But the SYT just smiled and ran off to get another waffle iron. Which, to my mounting frustration, she had difficulty finding. But she finally tracked one down and started ringing up the sale.

By now, Blondie had just two glasses left to wrap.

Go, sweet young thing, go! Work that computer, baby!

And indeed, the SYT did work fast. She rang up the sale with impressive speed. But then, just as she was about to hand the customer her waffle iron, I heard Blondie call out:

"Next, please."

I looked over and saw her glaring at me.

Rats. I was stuck. So be it. I refused to let her intimidate me. I took a deep breath and marched to the counter.

"I'd like to make a return," I said in my steeliest voice.

"No refunds," Blondie snapped, "without a—"

"Receipt?" I waved mine in triumph.

She took it from me with the tips of her fingers, eyeing my chocolate stain with disgust. Lord only knew what she was thinking.

"That's chocolate," I hastened to assure her.

"I'm sure it is," she said, glancing none too discreetly over the counter and down at my hips.

Oh, how I wanted to bop her with a Cookerie sauté pan.

Instead I handed her the corkscrew, still in its box.

She looked at it and wrinkled her nose job.

"That doesn't look like our gift wrap."

"Of course it's your gift wrap."

"No," Blondie said, with a taunting smile, "I don't think so."

And that's when I lost it. The woman was beyond impossible. She knew I bought the gift there. She'd wrapped it herself.

"I've had it with you, Nicole!" I shouted, squinting at her name tag. "You've given me nothing but grief ever since I first walked in the store. Just because I didn't drive up here in a Mercedes dressed in Armani doesn't mean I don't deserve to be treated with respect.

"I want my money back on this corkscrew," I said, ripping off the ribbons on the box, "and I want it now."

By now the store was hushed. Everyone was watching. I'd made a scene, but I didn't care. It was about time somebody told off this dreadful woman.

Grudgingly Blondie opened the box.

And then, to my surprise, she broke out into a small sly smile.

"I'd be happy to give you a refund on your corkscrew," she said. "But where is it?"

"What are you talking about? It's right there!"

"I don't think so," she said, holding up what looked like a giant metal thermometer.

"This"—her voice dripped disdain—"is something called a Sexometer."

Omigod. It was Walter's wedding gift! I must've grabbed it from the gift table by mistake. All those white gift wrappings looked so darn alike!

"Take your partner's sexual temperature," Blondie read aloud from a hang tag, "and work up a fever in bed."

The crowd tittered. Blondie was loving every minute of this.

"Shall I put it back in the box," she sneered, "or will you be using it?"

And then, in words far too graphic for your delicate ears, I told her exactly where she could put it.

Chapter 19

After slinking out of The Cookerie in disgrace, I ran to the arms of my good buddies, Ben & Jerry. Unlike most men, they know what to say to me when I'm hurting, those three little words that make my heart sing: *How many scoops?*

One dish of Chunky Monkey later, my spirits somewhat revived, I set off to see Patti's parents. I only hoped I'd have better luck getting my money from them than I did from Blondie.

The Devanes were home when I got there, still in mourning. Rosa led me to them in their den, a plush wood-paneled room with more leather accessories than a Mercedes showroom.

Daphna was sitting on one of the leather sofas, leafing through the latest issue of *Vogue*, her face its usual frozen mask. Was it grief, or was it Botox? Only her plastic surgeon knew for sure.

Conrad sat next to her, staring lifelessly at a plasma TV as the latest stock market numbers crawled on the bottom of the CNBC screen.

"Yes, Jaine?" Daphna said, more than a hint of impatience in her voice. "What is it?"

I couldn't just come right out and ask for my money. I had to ease into it.

"I wanted to tell you how sorry I am about Patti."

"Is that it?" she said, drumming her French tips on her magazine.

"Well, no. Actually, I was wondering if you've had a chance to look at the invoice I dropped in your mailbox."

"Oh, right," Conrad said, hauling himself up from the sofa. "I meant to write you a check but it slipped my mind. How much do we owe you?"

"Three thousand dollars."

Daphna sat up with a jolt.

"Three thousand dollars?" she squawked. "For a few measly lines of dialogue?"

Oh, for crying out loud, lady. You spend twice that much in an hour at Saks.

"That's the price Patti and I agreed on."

"We only have your word for that, don't we?"

"Now, Daphna." Her husband shot her a warning look. "I'm sure Ms. Austen is telling the truth.

"I'll go to my office and write that check," he said, giving me a conciliatory smile. "Have a seat and I'll be right back."

I took a seat and faced Daphna in an exceedingly awkward silence. Which was soon broken by the arrival of a yapping white ball of fur.

"Mamie!" I cried.

The next thing I knew, Patti's dog was in my lap and licking my face with wild abandon, no doubt remembering the carefree hours she'd spent romping in my garbage.

Daphna gritted her teeth in annoyance.

"Get lost, Mamie!"

The dog whimpered.

"Scram!" Daphna hissed. "I mean it."

Mamie reluctantly jumped off my lap and skittered out of the room.

"I can't bear looking at her." Daphna shook her head. "Too many memories of Patti."

"I'm sure you won't feel that way for long."

"You bet I won't. I'm shipping her off to the pound to-morrow."

"The pound?" I asked, horrified. "But if she's not adopted, she could be euthanized."

"That's not my problem," she said, dismissing Mamie's fate with a wave of her perfectly manicured hand. "All I know is I can't be bothered with her anymore."

And suddenly I was angry. Just because her daughter was dead didn't give her the right to throw away another life.

"Surely you must know someone who'd take her. She's such a cute little thing."

"You think she's so cute? You take her."

"All right," I found myself saying. "I will."

I knew there'd be hell to pay with Prozac, but I couldn't let Mamie go to the pound.

"Fine with me," she said, then called out for Rosa.

"Go pack Mamie's things," she said when the maid showed up at the door. "Jaine's going to take her. And Jaine, go help her," she added, almost as eager to be rid of me as the dog.

Thrilled to make my escape, I followed Rosa upstairs.

Patti's bubblegum pink room was just as I'd seen it on her wedding day. The only reminder of her gruesome death was police tape stretched across the French doors leading to the balcony.

"Here are Mamie's things," Rosa said, pulling out a large dresser drawer packed with doggie clothing.

Good heavens. The dog had more cashmere sweaters than I did.

"I'll get her suitcase," she said, reaching up to the top of the closet.

"Mamie has her own suitcase?"

"Monogrammed." She showed me the initials *MD* embroidered on a Gucci suitcase. Holy mackerel, now I'd seen everything.

I started packing Mamie's outfits, while Rosa gathered her bedding and toys.

"It's so nice of you to take her," she said. "I'm glad she's going to a loving home."

Needless to say, I didn't tell Rosa about the furious furball who'd be greeting us at the front door.

We were almost through gathering Mamie's things when the phone rang.

"I'd better get that," Rosa sighed. "Her ladyship doesn't like to wear herself out reaching for the telephone."

"That's okay," I said. "I'll finish up in here."

"Gracias." She smiled and hurried off.

Alone in the room, I figured I might as well take advantage of the opportunity to snoop around. It was a long shot, but I was hoping maybe I could unearth a clue that the police had somehow overlooked.

If only Patti's bubblegum pink walls could talk.

"Who came up here and tampered with the balcony?" I asked them. But all they seemed to say was, *Paint me!*

I peered out past the police tape onto the balcony. The railing hadn't been replaced, so all that was left was a bare stucco slab. Any bits of evidence had long since been swept away by either the cops or the wind.

Back in the room, I quickly rifled through Patti's drawers, but came up empty-handed.

With a sigh, I finished packing and was all set to go when I noticed Patti's Hermosa High yearbook on her night table.

Gad, I hadn't seen that thing since graduation. My parents lost mine in the move from Hermosa to Tampa Vistas. No great loss as far as I was concerned. I'd always hated my graduation picture, with my forced smile and Orphan Annie hair. It made my driver's license photo look like a *Cosmo* cover.

I had no real desire to look at it again, but like a dental patient who can't resist probing a sore tooth, I found myself walking over to check it out.

But I never did get to revisit the old me. Because just as I lifted the yearbook from the night table, a faded photo fluttered to the floor.

I picked it up and saw that it was a picture of Denise in her cheerleader outfit. Well, half of the outfit, anyway. I gulped back my surprise when I saw she wasn't wearing a stitch of clothing above her waist. Yep, she was totally topless—if you didn't count the butterfly tattooed on her shoulder.

Yikes. If that photo ever saw the light of day, Denise could kiss her political career good-bye.

Just as I'd suspected. Patti *had* been blackmailing her all these years. Which meant Denise had a strong motive to kill her.

At last. A bona fide Exhibit A!

I was so elated with my discovery that at first I didn't hear the sound of footsteps approaching. But at some point the clattering of Daphna's heels in the hallway broke into my consciousness.

I stashed the photo in my purse and had just put the yearbook back on the night table when Daphna popped her head in the door.

"Got everything you need?" she asked.

Yes, indeedie. And then some.

I drove home feeling a lot like Daniel must have felt before he sauntered into that lion's den.

Prozac was going to kill me when she saw Mamie.

I could just picture her reaction—the arched back, the swishing tail, the dramatic leap onto the top of the bookcase. No doubt about it. She'd be in full-tilt Drama Queen mode.

Mamie did not share my gloomy mood. She was perched

on the passenger seat, her head out the window, yapping a friendly hello to the passing fire hydrants. Poor thing had no idea she was leaving the lap of luxury for life in Economy Class.

"I sure hope you learn to like Alpo, kiddo."

All too soon, I pulled up in front of my duplex.

We were just getting out of the car when I saw Lance trotting up the street in his jogging shorts. Lance is one of those irritating people who actually enjoy working out.

"Hey dollface!" he said, joining us.

Naturally, he was talking to the dog.

"Where'd this cutie come from?" he asked, scooping her out of my arms.

"I inherited her from someone who died," I said, giving him the *Reader's Digest* version of events.

"Won't Prozac be upset if you bring home a dog?"

"That's putting it mildly. I'm fully expecting World War III to break out in my living room. Which is why I'm going to have to find another home for her."

"That shouldn't be hard," he said, scratching her behind the ears. "She's adorable."

"Hey," I said, a spark of hope igniting. "Why don't you take her?"

Mamie seemed to approve of this suggestion and began covering him with sloppy kisses.

"Clearly she's crazy about you."

"Actually," Lance said, gazing down at her, "I've always wanted a dog."

"Oh, Lance. She really is a sweetheart! So warm and loving and friendly. And hardly any trouble."

Notice how I didn't mention her penchant for rolling around in garbage. Which I didn't count as a flaw, since I was convinced Prozac put her up to it.

"I don't know," he hesitated. "It's all so sudden."

"She'd make a great date magnet," I said, revving up my sales pitch.

"I don't need a date magnet," he said, suddenly starry eyed. "I think at last I've found my soul mate."

I barely suppressed a groan. Lance is one of those incurable romantics who falls in love with the frequency of an NPR pledge drive.

"Remember Kevin?" he gushed. "The guy I met at the yogurt parlor? We're so totally on the same wave length. And not just about yogurt. About everything!"

I nodded through a few more beats of Isn't-Kevin-Wonderful chat, then got the conversation back on track.

"So what about Mamie?"

He looked down at the bundle of fur in his arms, then broke out into a smile. "Okay, I'll take her."

"Lance, you're an angel!"

I would've thrown my arms around him and covered him with kisses but Mamie beat me to it.

"I'll get her suitcase," I said, reaching into the Corolla.

"Omigod," Lance gasped. "Is that Gucci?"

"You bet. Monogrammed. And you should see her outfits. I never knew Versace made dog clothes."

"Oh, honey," he said, nuzzling Mamie's fur. "You're a girl after my own heart."

After settling Mamie at Lance's apartment, I trotted back to my own place, thrilled to have averted the wrath of Prozac.

"Hi, Pro!" I called out as I let myself in.

She looked up from where she was curled up on my sofa and sniffed.

I smell dog fur.

Her pink nose twitched indignantly.

And then, before she could get any closer, I raced to the shower to wash away all traces of The Other Woman.

YOU'VE GOT MAIL

NOBEL PRIZE WINNER ABDUCTED FROM AIRPORT

Famed Italian physicist and Nobel Prize winner Enrico Fac-ciobene, whom Stephen Hawking has called "one of the keenest analytical minds of our generation," was abducted from Tampa International Airport last night by what witnesses described as a deranged attorney.

Facciobene was scheduled to begin a research grant at the University of Tampa. But when representatives of the university arrived at the airport to pick him up, they saw him being forcibly dragged to a white late-model Toyota Camry.

Professor Susan MacDonald described the abductor as a balding man in his sixties wearing an If At First You Don't Succeed, Sue, Sue Again *T-shirt.*

"This crazy fellow tore out of the airport and raced to his car, which was illegally parked in a white zone," said MacDonald, "dragging poor Signor Facciobene against his will."

Any witnesses with information about the abduction should contact Det. John Hill at (813) 555-9876.

To: Jausten
From: Shoptillyoudrop

Can't write much now. I'm off to bail Daddy out of jail.

More later—

Mom

To: Jausten
From: Shoptillyoudrop
Subject: The Wrong Man!

Well, I'm back, and you'll never believe what happened.

Daddy picked up the wrong man at the airport!

I don't know how he could have possibly made such a ridiculous mistake. The man looked nothing like Roberto's picture. I knew the minute he walked in the house it wasn't him.

Daddy always was bad at recognizing people. I'll never forget the time he asked a waitress at Howard Johnson's for her autograph because he swore she was Meryl Streep. I said, "Hank, what on earth would Meryl Streep be doing waiting tables here in Tampa?" He insisted it was her, said she was probably "researching a role."

But I'm rambling, aren't I? Getting back to Signor Facciobene. That's the man Daddy abducted, a famous scientist from Italy. I could tell the poor man was upset. He kept shouting "Hiya! Hiya!" It turns out he was trying to say "Hyatt." That's where he was supposed to be staying, but of course we didn't know that.

I said to your father, "Hank, this isn't Roberto." And he said, "Of course it is; he looks just like his photo," and I said, "I'm the one who dated him; I should know who he is for heaven's sake!"

"Well, if he isn't Roberto," Daddy asked, "who the heck is he?"

And just then I happened to look over at the TV, which I'd turned on while I was setting the table. You know how I like to have the TV on to keep me company when I'm doing chores around the house. Anyhow, there on the TV was a news bulletin with Signor Facciobene's picture, saying how a world-famous Nobel Prize winner had been abducted from the airport by a crazy man in an *If At First You Don't Succeed, Sue, Sue Again* T-shirt!

"Good gracious, Hank!" I said. "You've kidnapped a Nobel Prize winner! How could you??"

But Daddy never did get a chance to answer my question because just then the doorbell rang. And there on our doorstep, where all the neighbors could see them, I'm sure, were two uniformed policemen!

Daddy started babbling that it was all an innocent mistake, that he hadn't meant to kidnap anybody, that he thought he was picking up his wife's boyfriend. You can imagine how red my face turned at that.

But it turned out they weren't here about Signor Facciobene. "We've come to investigate a claim of stolen property," one of them said. "An overdue library book."

Can you believe it? They were here about Daddy's silly library book!

At which point Signor Facciobene came running up to them crying "Aiuto! Aiuto!" which apparently is Italian for "help." Of course the police recognized him right away, and faster than you can say "Arrivederci, Roma," they were carting Daddy off to jail.

And just as they were driving off, you'll never guess who pulled up in a taxi. The real Roberto! I have to admit, he didn't look much like the photo he sent; that picture must've been taken years ago. He's put on quite a few pounds since then. But he's still as sweet as ever and was kind enough to come down to police headquarters with me. After they called in a translator, Roberto explained what happened and they let Daddy go.

Then the three of us all had a lovely dinner at Applebee's because I'm sorry to say in all the ruckus of Daddy getting arrested, my eggplant parmagiana got burned to a crisp.

Well, that's it for now, darling. I'm off to bed. Which reminds me. I sent you some fabulous leopard throw pillows to go with your new comforter set. They've got a few teeny rhinestones on the leopard's nose which may be a trifle garish, but I'm sure you can snip them off.

Much love—

Mom

To: Jausten
From: DaddyO
Subject: Little Mix-up

I suppose Mom wrote you about that little mix-up at the airport. It was a perfectly understandable mistake. After all, the fellow kept saying Hiya! Hiya! I thought he was saying hello. The only reason I dragged him to the car was because I was parked in the white zone and I didn't want to get a ticket.

And I don't care what your mother says, the man was the spitting image of Roberto's picture. I happen to have an amazing gift for recognizing people. Why, I once saw Meryl Streep waiting tables at HoJo's!

How many people can say that?

Love and hugs from,

Daddy

Chapter 20

I drove over to Denise's law office the next day, my mind reeling over my parents' e-mails. Can you believe Daddy kidnapped a Nobel Prize winner? This was worse than the time he set fire to the Tampa Vistas clubhouse. I'm telling you, the man should be declared a National Disaster Area. How he's made it this far without a prison record is beyond me.

But I couldn't think about Daddy. Not now. I had to stay focused on the case and confront Denise with my Topless Cheerleader discovery.

After parking my Corolla deep in the bowels of Denise's high rise, I took a series of escalators up to the lobby and then boarded the elevator to her sky-high office.

I went over my plan of attack as I rode up. I'd barge into her office and catch her off guard. Then I'd flash the Topless Cheerleader photo and watch her face crumple in dismay. Tears streaming down her face, she'd admit that Patti had been blackmailing her and that she'd resorted to murder to put a stop to it.

With any luck, I'd be walking out of her office with a signed confession.

But things didn't exactly go according to plan.

For starters, I didn't barge into Denise's office. Her gargoyle secretary (a woman with biceps the size of Easter hams) kept me cooling my heels for thirty-five minutes before she finally allowed me to go in.

"Hello, Jaine," Denise greeted me, not the least bit startled, having had thirty-five minutes to prepare for my appearance. "How can I help you?"

"Take a look at what I found in Patti's yearbook." I said, trying my best to send out Tough Girl vibes.

I whipped the topless cheerleader photo from my purse and showed it to her. Sad to say, she didn't crumple in dismay. No tearful confessions ensued. Nope. She just threw back her head and laughed.

"Patti still had that silly thing?"

And suddenly my theory that Patti had been blackmailing Denise didn't seem quite as compelling as it had thirty seconds ago.

I plowed ahead anyway.

"I think Patti was using this picture to keep you under her thumb. That's why you stayed friendly with her all these years. You were afraid not to. But when you decided to run for office, you couldn't risk having her spill the beans about your topless past."

"Are you saying I'm the one who sabotaged that balcony?"

She wasn't laughing anymore.

"Yes. That's exactly what I'm saying."

She got up from her chair, reed thin in a pinstriped pantsuit, and walked around her desk to face me.

"I already told you, Jaine," she said in an even voice. "I stayed in Patti's life for one reason only. I felt sorry for her. I don't run scared. Not from anyone. Not Patti. Not the voters. And certainly not you."

Well, that certainly knocked the stuffing out of my piñata.

"As for that silly 'blackmail' picture, lest you forget, I'm running for office in the state of California. A topless picture of me in my cheerleader days will probably win me the election."

I had to hand it to her. If she was bluffing, she was doing

one hell of a job. Why couldn't I ever stand up to people like that? I usually fold after the first dirty look. Like I did with Kyle Potter.

And like I was about to do then.

"Hey, it was just a wacky theory," I said, backing out of the room. "I get 'em all the time. Doesn't mean it's true. Well, I've wasted enough of your valuable time. Must dash. Great seeing you! Rah, rah, Hermosa, and all that."

I scooted out of her office and made my way to the elevator, minus my backbone. I really had to work on my confrontational skills. But in the cold light of Denise's icy glare, my blackmail theory seemed pretty lame.

On the other hand, she could've been bluffing. Maybe her bravado was just an act. All I knew for sure was that Denise was one cool cookie. The woman had the cojones of a Beverly Hills real estate broker.

I sure as heck didn't envy the poor soul who was running against her.

The elevator ride down to the lobby took forever, stopping at what seemed like every other floor. Before long, the tiny space was jammed with $500-an-hour attorneys, packed together like sardines in testosterone.

At last the elevator doors dinged open. I made my way across the travertine marble lobby to the escalators that led down to the garage. They, too, were crowded when I got on, but by the time I got to the peon level of the garage where I'd parked, I was the only one still on.

I started the long trek to my car, which was parked in the spot I always seemed to get stuck with—the one as far as possible from the escalators.

It was dark and creepy down in peon-land. You'd think they'd spring for some decent lighting in a ritzy building like this. Instead they had puny 40-watt bulbs casting ominous shadows wherever I looked.

Suddenly I felt uneasy, as if some unknown danger were lurking in the shadows. It told myself I was being silly. It was just this murder business that had me on edge.

Nevertheless I trotted the rest of the way to my car, eager to get out of this dungeon and back into the light of day. At last I saw my trusty Corolla. With a sigh of relief I ran to its dinged side.

I'd opened the door and was just about to get in when I noticed a flyer stuck under the windshield:

LOSE WEIGHT FAST!
Seven-Day Wonder
DIET!
Call (323) 555-7676 for details

A jolt of fear ran down my spine.

Not at the thought of going on a diet, although that's never a pleasant prospect.

No, what sent that tingle down my spine was the fact that someone had scratched out the "T" in diet, changing it to:

DIE!

Was this a threat from the killer? Her way of telling me to mind my own business?

Just then I heard the sound of high heels clicking on the cement. I turned and saw a woman heading toward the escalator alcove. A reed thin brunette. I gulped when I saw what she was wearing. *A pinstriped suit!* I'd just seen that same pantsuit not five minutes ago.

My God, it was Denise!

So she *had* been bluffing in her office. She *was* the killer. She must've taken an express elevator and put the note under my windshield to scare me off the case. After the way

I'd caved in her office, she probably figured it would be easy to put the fear of God in me. She was right of course. I was a tad terrified. But I'd be damned if I'd let her intimidate me.

"Denise!" I called out.

She went on walking.

I started to run after her, and at the sound of my footsteps, she started running, too. The chase was on—but I had the advantage. I was wearing running shoes while she was stuck with wobbly designer heels.

That is, I thought I had the advantage. For a woman in three-inch stilettos, she was pretty darn fast. As I went puffing after her, weaving in and out between luxury cars, I cursed myself for not going to the gym more often. Or ever, if you want to get technical.

But eventually I managed to narrow the gap between us. I'd almost caught up with her and was all set to pounce when I heard the earsplitting sound of brakes squealing.

I looked up and saw that I had come *thisclose* to being mowed down by an SUV. An angry blonde in designer sunglasses shouted at me through her open window.

"Are you crazy, darting out in front of my car like that? I could've killed you."

"You'll have to wait your turn," I shouted as I dashed into the escalator alcove where Denise had disappeared.

By now she was halfway to the top of the stairs. I was just about to leap on after her when out of nowhere a young mother with a baby stroller jutted in front of me. And it wasn't just any baby stroller. The woman had twins! Talk about inconsiderate. Couldn't she sense I was chasing a killer? And what the heck was she doing bringing toddlers to an office building? There was no way I was going to get past her and her wide-bodied stroller.

And so I did what millions of drunken fraternity boys have

been doing since time immemorial. I went up the Down escalator.

Trust me, it's not easy. Now I knew what a salmon felt like at spawning time.

"Stop that woman!" I shouted as I struggled against the current of the downward moving steps. "She's the Bridezilla Killer!"

But my fellow escalatorians just looked at me like I was nuts. Can't say as I blame them. I was, after all, a woman in a *Cuckoo for Cocoa Puffs* T-shirt going up the Down escalator.

Pushing my way past the downstream passengers, I finally made it to the top. This time, with no pesky strollers impeding my progress, I leaped onto the next escalator and took the steps two at a time.

"It's no use, Denise!" I called out as she got off the escalator. "I know you killed Patti."

In a final burst of speed, I attacked her from behind and shoved her up against a wall.

"Please don't hurt me!" she cried.

Funny, that didn't sound like Denise.

"Take my money!" she pleaded. "It's in my purse."

By now a crowd had formed around us. The young mother with the twins, I saw, had stopped to take in the show.

"What's going on here?" asked a concerned bizguy, shooting me a dirty look.

My captive turned to face me, and with a sinking sensation, I saw that it wasn't Denise. Not even close. She was a fresh-scrubbed gal with freckles and rosy cheeks (no doubt a fear-induced cardiac flush).

Yes, folks. The "killer" I'd just chased across the parking garage and up two flights of escalators was a perfectly innocent stranger.

* * *

Ten minutes later I was in the bunker-like offices of the Century City police begging my innocent victim not to press charges.

How could I have been so stupid? Chasing her down just because she was a skinny woman in a designer suit. For crying out loud, this was L.A., where nine out of ten women are skinny and in designer suits. And why hadn't it occurred to me before I went sprinting off on my wild goose chase that Denise would have had no way of knowing where I'd parked my car?

I'd thought Daddy was nuts, bringing home the wrong guy from the airport. Daddy didn't hold a candle to me in the Stupid Mistakes department. I was a disgrace to private eyes everywhere. And freelance writers, too.

"I'm so sorry," I said to my victim. "You see, I got this flyer on my windshield, and the *T* in *DIET* had been crossed out so all it said was *DIE* and I thought you were the killer."

The cop who'd driven us over on his golf cart looked up from the notes he was taking and shot me a piercing look.

"What killer?"

Oh, crud. The last thing I wanted to do was tell him I was investigating Patti's murder. Not after having just attacked an innocent citizen. Surely that would lead to all sorts of pesky questions about whether I was licensed to be a P.I., which of course I wasn't.

"Did I say *the* killer? I meant *a* killer. I just thought she was a dangerous person and wanted to make a citizen's arrest."

"Talk about overreacting," my victim piped up. "I got the same flyer on my windshield, and I didn't go attacking anyone."

She took out a flyer from her purse, and sure enough, the *T* in her *DIET* had been crossed out, too.

At that moment, the door opened and a couple of security guards came in, hauling two sullen teenage boys.

"These kids were hired to put diet flyers under windshields," said one of the guards, "and they thought it would be funny to cross off the *T*, so it said *DIE*. Scared a lot of people."

"I know all about it," the desk cop said, rolling his eyes. "Just let me finish up with these women and I'll get to the kids."

Finally, after I promised to write free resumes for all three of my victim's children, she agreed not to press charges.

The cop let me go with a stern warning about overreacting and a not-so-subtle suggestion that I seek psychiatric counseling.

I was just about to leave his office when I looked up at a TV mounted on the wall. There on the news was a picture of Julio, the Devanes' gardener.

I raced over and turned up the sound just in time to hear the anchorman saying, "—found dead in a ravine, his body riddled with bullets."

Needless to say, I was glued to the news that night. Normally the death of a gardener wouldn't rate much coverage, but because of Julio's connection with the Devanes, he was granted his fifteen minutes of posthumous fame.

All the local stations ran with the story. According to their accounts, Julio had been dead for at least two days, killed in what the police were saying was most likely a drug deal gone bad.

A drug deal? I didn't think so.

I'm no expert on drugs (unless you consider Chunky Monkey a narcotic), but I had a hard time picturing timid little Julio in a dark alley forking over hard cash for white powder.

The way I figured it, Julio was offed because he'd seen the killer. Somehow she found out that there'd been an eyewitness to her crime and tracked poor Julio down. Even though he hadn't been able to give a clear description of her, she was taking no chances that someday he might be able to identify her.

Zapping from one newscast to another, I saw that one enterprising station had sent out a news team to the East L.A. apartment building where Julio had rented a room. The reporter tried to talk to the manager of the building, a tank of a woman in a floral muumuu and a headful of rollers. But— in a moment I was certain would never appear on the reporter's demo real—she chased him away with a broom and a string of bleeped-out curses.

A formidable woman, indeed. I wouldn't want to be late with my rent in her building.

But maybe she'd seen or heard something that would lead me to Julio's killer. Maybe she'd even seen the murderer. I needed to talk to her and pump her for information.

As the frightened reporter scurried to the safety of his news van, I saw a sign on the apartment lawn:

LUCILLE ARMS. VACANCY

Lucille could have been the name of the woman in the muumuu, of course. And the building could have been named for her pendulous arms. But I didn't think so. A quick trip to Mapquest, and I discovered a street in East L.A. called Lucille Avenue. Like so many apartments, Lucille Arms was probably named after the street it was built on.

It shouldn't be too hard to drive along Lucille Avenue until I spotted it.

Now all I had to do was think of a way to approach the manager without getting attacked with a broomstick.

Then I remembered the VACANCY sign on the lawn. And I knew exactly how to get an audience with the muumuu-clad manager.

First thing tomorrow morning, I would go apartment hunting.

Chapter 21

Lucille Avenue was a lot longer than it looked on the map. When I passed my third bodega it was clear I was in a predominantly Hispanic section of town.

Crawling along at fifteen miles an hour, scanning the streets for Lucille Arms, I stood out like a gringo sore thumb. Drivers behind me honked impatiently, but I couldn't risk going faster or I'd miss Julio's apartment.

At last I found it—a squat two-story building with security bars on the windows and a patch of weeds masquerading as a front lawn.

I parked my ancient Corolla (which was right at home on the streets of East L.A.) and headed up the front path.

Reassured to see the VACANCY sign still up, I rang the manager's buzzer. A blast of static came on the line, and then a hoarse "Yeah? Whaddaya want?"

"I'm here about your rental unit."

"Hold on. I'll be right out."

I peered past the security bars on the glass door into a musty hallway with a bare overhead lightbulb. The same woman I'd seen on the news came out of one of the apartments, carrying her trusty broom. She waddled to the front door in the muumuu she'd worn yesterday, her hair still in rollers. Why did I get the feeling those rollers had been in her hair since 1987?

She opened the door warily, a cigarette dangling from her lips. With beady raisin eyes and a most unfortunate mustache, she looked a lot scarier in person than she had on TV. And that was pretty darn scary.

"You the one who buzzed me?"

I nodded mutely.

"Why the hell do you want to rent a place here? It's all Mexicans."

"That's okay with me. I think Hispanic people are just fine."

"Well bully for you," she sneered. "Somebody get this girl a humanitarian award."

Mexicans, I liked. Her, I didn't.

Her beady eyes narrowed in suspicion.

"You're not a reporter, are you?"

"No," I blinked, all innocence. "I'm not a reporter."

"You a hooker?"

"Only on my lunch hour."

Of course I didn't say that. I assured her I was an upright citizen who paid my rent with clockwork regularity.

"I still don't understand why you want to live here," she said. "You'd be the only white person here except for me."

"Well, I work nearby and I thought the rent would be reasonable."

"It's three hundred a month. That reasonable enough?"

"Sounds great!"

"No pets, no loud noise, no smoking." This uttered with an inch of ash dangling from her cigarette.

"Fine with me," I chirped.

"You sure you're not a reporter?"

"No, I'm not a reporter."

She peered out behind me and, convinced that there were no cameramen lurking in the bushes, she motioned me inside.

I followed her down a dank hallway that smelled of onion and mildew.

"It sure would be nice to have another white person living here," she said, as she waddled along with her broom. "I'm tired of habla-ing espanol all the time. We could hang out together. Knock back a few beers and watch *Friday Night Smackdown* on my plasma TV."

What an appalling prospect.

"Well, here it is," she said, opening one of the doors.

We stepped into a barren cell of a room. Floral wallpaper that had been picked out sometime in the Truman administration was peeling from the walls. One tiny barred window looked out onto a scenic view of the neighbor's trash cans.

"Comes completely furnished," she said, gesturing to a sagging twin bed and a scarred wooden dresser. "Here's your kitchen." She waved to a hot plate sitting atop a mini-fridge. And here's the bathroom."

I peeked into a closet-sized room so moldy, I was surprised moss wasn't growing on the faucets.

"So what do you think?" she asked, giving me her impersonation of a smile. "Wanna take it? First and last months' rent due in advance. In cash."

Whoa. This was going way too fast. I had to change the subject or I'd wind up with a five-year lease on my hands.

"Hey, wait a minute," I said, as if recognizing her for the first time. "Didn't I see you on the news last night? In the story about the gardener who was killed?"

"That was me all right," she muttered. "Damn reporters, ringing my bell in the middle of *Judge Judy*. Made me miss the verdict."

"Gee," I gushed. "You're so much more attractive in person!"

Why I wasn't struck down by lightning for that whopper I'll never know.

"Oh?" she preened, flashing me a tobacco-stained grin. "So you know about Julio, the guy who got mowed down?"

"Yes, I heard all about it. Was this his room?"

"Yeah," she nodded ruefully.

I casually opened one of his dresser drawers, hoping maybe they hadn't yet been cleaned out. But no luck. Totally empty.

"You don't mind renting a place whose previous tenant took a round of bullets in the gut, do you?" she asked. "Some people are queasy that way."

"As long as it didn't happen in the room."

"No, it didn't happen here," she assured me. "Those bloodstains on the wall are from a previous tenant. Julio was shot in a ravine miles from here."

"Poor guy," I tsked. "I heard on the news it was a drug deal gone bad."

"Who knows? He sure didn't seem like a druggie to me. Sober as a judge every time I saw him. Paid his rent on time. That's all I cared about."

"Did any women ever come to visit him at his apartment?"

"Why the hell do you need to know that?" she barked, her suspicions aroused.

I put on my tap shoes and did some fast dancing.

"Well," I vamped, "the last place I rented, the former tenant had a bunch of ex-girlfriends who were always banging on my door in the middle of the night. And I don't want to live through that again."

Thank heavens, she bought it.

"Nah. No women ever showed up here. Julio had a wife and family back in Mexico. Sent them money every month. No women, no music, no nothing. Guy was quiet as a mouse. Hardly ever talked to him. Except the day he gave his thirty days' notice. Then he was real chatty."

"He was planning to move?"

"Yeah, he must've come into some money. Said he was going to be on easy street."

"He came into some money?" Very interesting indeed. "Do you know from who?"

Now her eyes got all beady again.

"Why are you asking so many questions? You sure you're not a reporter?"

"No, I swear I'm not a reporter. I'm just inquisitive, I guess."

"Yeah, well. I'm inquisitive, too. I wanna know if you want the damn apartment or not."

"Um. Sure. You don't mind pets, do you? My cat is very quiet, and the vet says her incontinence should clear up any day now."

"You got a cat?" Her double chin quivered in irritation.

"Yes, didn't I mention that? That's why I'm moving. My current landlord is so heartless. Just because of a few 'accidents' on the carpeting. You'd think nobody ever had a cat with diarrhea before."

"What are you wasting my time for? I already told you— no pets."

"Did you? Gosh, I was so excited about seeing the room, I guess I didn't hear."

"Beat it, girlie. I'm missing *The Price Is Right*."

And before she could reach for her broom, I was gone.

"So what do you think, Prozac? Where was Julio getting that money?"

I was stretched out in my bathtub, up to my neck in strawberry-scented bubbles, mulling over my meeting with Julio's Godzilla apartment manager.

Prozac gazed down at me from her perch atop the toilet tank.

"Julio told Ms. Muumuu that he was going to be on easy street, that he was coming into a lot of money. So where was it coming from?"

Prozac thought this over and then, as she so often does when faced with a thorny problem, began licking her privates.

It looked like I was flying solo on this one.

Where, I asked myself, would a guy like Julio get a lot of dough?

The first answer that sprang to mind was blackmail.

Maybe, contrary to what he told the cops, Julio got a good look at the woman who was out on the balcony. Maybe he knew exactly who she was and had been blackmailing her, threatening to expose her unless she coughed up some dough. And maybe, instead, she coughed up a round of bullets.

I'd always thought it was odd that Julio wasn't able to give a clearer description of the killer. Surely he would've been able to identify something about her.

But who was he blackmailing?

It had to be someone with money. Which let Normalynne and Cheryl off the hook. Neither of them could finance a life on welfare, let alone easy street.

My leading suspect was Denise. From the looks of her office, she was rolling in big bucks. If indeed she'd knocked off Patti to keep her from blabbing about her topless cheerleader past, surely she'd have no compunctions about blowing poor Julio away. Denise was a tough cookie; quite capable, I thought, of firing off a round of bullets between court cases.

And of course there was Eleanor Potter. Although not megarich, the Potters certainly had money. Maybe Eleanor didn't go to Patti's room to look for sex tapes, but to sabotage the balcony with her husband's power drill. And then, when Julio threatened to expose her, she'd packed a pistol in her sweatsuit and used him for target practice.

And what about Veronica? I'd bet she was making a pretty penny from her catering biz. True, I had a hard time believing that someone who could cook such heavenly empanadas was capable of murder, but I had to leave my taste buds out of this equation and look at things objectively. It was possible she knocked off both Patti and Julio to keep things cooking at Hubbard's Cupboard.

I was lying there in the tub, thinking about my suspects—and not incidentally about Veronica's empanadas—when the phone rang. I groaned as I heard Walter Barnhardt's nasal whine on my answering machine, reminding me that tonight was the night of the Hermosa High reunion and that I was to meet him at 8 o'clock in front of the buffet table, in case I'd forgotten.

No I hadn't forgotten. Mainly because this was his seventh message in three days. I didn't tell you about the others because I wanted to spare you the aggravation. (Not many authors are this considerate; just remember that the next time you're in the bookstore wondering what to get.)

With a weary sigh, I hauled myself from the tub and trudged to the bedroom to get dressed.

I reached into my closet for the black cocktail dress I'd worn to Patti's wedding. I'd been meaning to take it to the cleaners but had never gotten around to it. It still smelled faintly of the flaming rum punch that sloshed on it when I'd set fire to Walter's toupee.

Oh, well. It would have to do.

As I proceed to rummage in my dresser drawer for a pair of unclawed panty hose, my mind drifted to thoughts of the night ahead.

I'd always harbored a secret fantasy of showing up at a reunion one day, cool and sophisticated and fifteen pounds thinner, my hair miraculously straight, my thighs miraculously toned, a hunky yet sensitive escort at my side. My fellow classmates would gaze at me, awed, as I sailed into the room, laughing gaily, a far cry from the goofy gal they'd last seen crash landing on Principal Seawright's lap.

And now, here I was—about to show up with Walter Barnhardt and his mail order toupee.

But I had to remind myself why I'd agreed to go to the reunion with Walter in the first place. It was the least I could do after all the pain I'd caused him in high school. Was I so shallow that I cared what a bunch of people I hadn't seen in nearly two decades thought of me? Was I still stuck in that adolescent need to impress my peers?

Well, actually, yes.

But it was high time I got over it. I'd go to the reunion and show Walter a good time. I owed him that much.

It was a new, nobler me that fished out a pair of only marginally clawed panty hose from my dresser drawer and finished dressing. I'd just spritzed my final spritz of cologne and was checking myself out in the mirror when I heard a knock at my front door.

I opened it to find Lance standing on my doorstep with Mamie in his arms. Along with her suitcase, toys, and doggie bed at his feet.

"Oh, Jaine," he wailed. "I feel terrible."

"What's wrong? Is Mamie sick?"

"No, but Kevin is. I didn't know it, but he's allergic to dogs. He's in my apartment now and just broke out in hives. I feel awful about this," he said, thrusting Mamie into my arms, "but I can't keep her."

"But you were so crazy about her."

"I am crazy about her. But how can I keep Mamie if Kevin's going to get hives every time he sees her? Sooner or later, we're going to move in together, and what would happen then? I'd rather give her up now, before I fall any more in love with her than I already am."

Tears welled in his eyes. I could tell this was breaking his heart.

"That's okay," I said. "I understand."

"Good-bye, sweetheart." He leaned over and kissed Mamie on her nose, then headed back to his place.

"Don't worry," I told Mamie as I took her into my apartment. "We'll find you a good home yet."

Mamie, not the least bit worried, was lapping at my face, happy to be back with the lady with the smelly garbage pail.

And even happier to be back with Prozac. She took one look at her long lost friend, sprawled out on the sofa, and began barking excitedly.

The feeling, I regret to say, was not mutual.

Prozac glared at me through slitted eyes.

Her again? I thought we'd established this was a one-pet household.

With that, she stood up and arched her back. Never a good sign. Nor was the hiss that followed.

What the heck was I going to do now? I couldn't possibly go off to the reunion and leave them alone together lest I come home and find poor Mamie's bloodied body embedded with cat claws.

There was no doubt about it. I'd have to keep them separated. I settled Mamie in my bedroom with her toys and doggie bed and turned on the TV.

"Look, sweetie. A *Lassie* marathon on TV Land. Won't that be fun? Now you have a good time and I'll be back before you know it."

I gave her a kiss good-bye and closed the bedroom door firmly behind me.

She let out a sad little whimper, but I had to hang tough.

"It's for your own good," I called out to her. "Trust me. You don't want to mess with Prozac. She's like a pit bull with hairballs."

I headed to the living room where Prozac was now sprawled out on my computer keyboard.

How come she gets to watch TV and all I get is this crummy screensaver?

"Just behave yourself," I said.

Then I grabbed my car keys and took off for my second and absolutely final date with Walter Barnhardt.

Chapter 22

The Hermosa High gym still smelled the same. They could drape it with crepe paper and string it with balloons, but it still smelled like varnish and sweat socks to me.

A tuxedo-clad combo was stationed under one of the basketball hoops, playing dance music. But it was too early in the evening for alcohol to have loosened inhibitions, so only a few couples were dancing.

I looked around for Walter, but he wasn't there yet.

Neither were Denise or Cheryl. Which didn't surprise me. Denise had surely outgrown her hometown classmates. And I seriously doubted Cheryl would want her fellow grads to see how low she'd fallen.

One person I did see, however, was Principal Seawright. His hair had gone silver, and he walked with a cane, but other than that he looked pretty darn good for a guy who had to be in his eighties. He was chatting with a bunch of alums, honor roll kids, no doubt. Cringing at the memory of our last encounter, I vowed to avoid him at all costs.

I headed over to the buffet table and helped myself to a mini-quiche. Gooey with cheese and studded with chunks of ham, it was absolute heaven. I could not possibly allow myself to eat more than one.

As I stood there shoveling it down, I heard snippets of conversation around me. Everyone was buzzing about Patti's death.

What a way to go.

Impaled on a statue of cupid.

Ugh! How gruesome!

I plucked another mini-quiche off the platter—this was the last one, absolutely—and popped it in my mouth just in time to hear:

They say that one of the guests turned up at the wedding with a paid escort and tried to pass him off as her fiancé.

You're kidding!

I'm serious. Turned out the guy was really a male stripper.

My God. Who would be so desperate?

Before they could look around and wonder if the woman with the quiche in her mouth was the desperado in question, I scooted down to the other end of the buffet table. Where the hell was Walter, anyway?

At last I saw him scurrying across the room. As he got closer I tried not to gasp. I know it defies rational belief, but his new toupee was even worse than his old one.

His last one had looked like a dead hamster. This one looked alive. I swear, I thought I saw it wink at me.

"So how do you like my new hair?" he asked, with a pathetically hopeful smile.

Somehow I managed to choke out the words, "Very nice."

"Who says you can't get a good hairpiece for $29.99?" he beamed.

"Look." He took out another equally hideous hank of animal fur from his jacket pocket. "I brought a spare. Just in case you get anywhere near a match, haha."

I smiled weakly as he shoved it back in his pocket.

"And see what else I brought," he said, holding out a box.

I just hoped it wasn't Cheerios.

"A corsage!"

He took out a corsage the size of a funeral wreath.

"Why, thank you, Walter. That's very sweet."

And it was sweet of him. I just wished it didn't look like he'd picked it off a grave site.

"Let me pin it on you."

"No, I'll do it," I said, not wanting him anywhere near my chest.

With some difficulty I managed to pin it on my shoulder strap. I'm surprised it didn't break the strap.

"Gosh, you look pretty," he said. "Want to dance?"

Along with Principal Seawright, dancing was high on my Must Avoid At All Costs list. The last thing I wanted to do was revisit the scene of my prom night humiliation.

"I don't think so, Walter."

"Oh." He was disappointed, I could tell, but nothing was going to get me out on that dance floor.

"Okay, then," he said. "How about a drink from the bar?"

Now he was talking. At last my eyes lit up with genuine enthusiasm.

"Oh, yes, thanks. A white wine would be lovely."

"Don't go away," he said, shooting his finger at me like a gun, in a gesture that was considered passé back in high school. "I'll be back."

And then he trotted off to get on line at the bar.

I was standing there, debating about whether I should go back for my third (okay, fourth) mini-quiche, when I heard:

"Jaine Austen! Is that you?"

I turned to see a handsome dark-haired guy in a tweed jacket.

"It's me. Dylan Janovici."

Oh, Lord. My druggie prom date. I had to admit, I was surprised at how good he looked. I would've thought by this time he'd have ingested so many illegal substances he'd be incapable of speech.

But no, he had an intelligent gleam in his eyes and turned out to be perfectly articulate.

"How've you been?" he asked.

"Fine."

"Interesting corsage," he said, nodding at my chest.

"Yes, I think in a former life it was a centerpiece at a Bar Mitzvah."

"You know, Jaine," he said, flashing me a most disarming smile. "I really owe you an apology for the way I behaved on our prom date. What a jerk I was back then. I'm so sorry for showing up at your house stoned."

"Oh, that's okay."

"I still can't believe those crazy dance moves of mine. Do you know I threw my back out that night? I guess it must have happened when I tried to flip you over my shoulder."

Oh, great. The poor guy broke his back trying to lift me and my mega-thighs.

"I had to spend three months in traction."

"That's awful, Dylan. I'm so sorry."

"Don't be. It was the best thing that ever happened to me. Trapped in bed, I started reading. I never did get around to Nietzsche," he said, smiling at the memory of the phony "book" where he stored his stash of weed, "but I did read James Joyce and Edith Wharton and P. G. Wodehouse. And all of Jane Austen, I might add."

This said with another most disarming smile.

"Now I'm an English professor at USC. And I owe it all to dancing with you."

An English professor! My high school fantasies of Dylan as a sensitive intelligent guy had actually come true.

"So what about you?" he asked, as if he really wanted to know. "What's going on in your life?"

I told him I was a writer, carefully omitting the fact that I spent much of my working life writing about Toiletmasters' fine line of Ever-Flush commodes.

"You married?" he asked, a twinkle in his eye.

"Nope."

"Me, neither."

"Oh?" I tried not to break out in a happy little jig.

"In that case," he grinned, "I'd like to make up for my bad behavior at the prom by taking you to dinner. Can I call you some time?"

Before I could shout a resounding *yesyesyesyesyes!*, we were interrupted.

"Hi, hon!"

I turned to see Walter and his hamster hair.

"I got your drink." He handed me my wine and at the same time clamped his arm around my waist in a steely grip.

"You two together?" Dylan asked, his smile stiffening.

"No, no," I said, wrenching myself free from Walter's grasp. "We're just friends. *Right, Walter?*"

"That's right," Walter said, with a suggestive leer. "Just friends. Wink wink. Nudge, nudge."

"Well, catch you later," Dylan said weakly, and before I could stop him he disappeared into the crowd.

The minute he was gone I whirled on Walter and shot him a look so smoldering, I was surprised his toupee didn't spontaneously combust.

"For crying out loud, Walter. I thought we agreed. This night was supposed to be strictly platonic. We are *just friends*. No arms around my waist. No wink wink, nudge nudge. Understand?"

"I understand," he said softly, looking down at the floor.

"Really, if you tell one more person we're a couple, I'm leaving."

He looked up, alarmed.

"Don't do that. I'll be good. I promise."

And he was.

He spent the next hour or so doing a reasonable impersonation of a human being. He didn't touch me once as we circulated among the crowd. Nor did he leer or call me "hon." We stopped to talk with the few people I remembered (Joey

Romano, the class clown, I was interested to learn, was now a funeral director) and spent a stultifying twenty minutes chatting about the good old days solving equations with the members of Walter's old math club.

"Want to get some chow?" Walter asked when we'd run out of former acquaintances.

He didn't get an argument from me on that one. It had been a while since my mini-quiches and I was feeling a bit peckish.

I restrained myself, however, from piling my plate with food in case Dylan came back to join us. Just a few Swedish meatballs and some macaroni salad. I did not want him to think I was the kind of woman who needed a forklift to carry her buffet plate. I am that kind of woman, but Dylan didn't need to know that.

Walter and I grabbed two seats at one of the tables scattered around the gym, and I spent the next half hour dutifully listening to him yak about the wacky world of insurance actuaries.

True, my mind wandered a tad as he yammered on. Every once in a while I'd see Dylan out of the corner of my eye, making the rounds. For a few disconcerting moments I saw him deep in an animated discussion with a most attractive blonde. I kept hoping he'd stop at our table, but he never did.

Somehow I managed to keep my eyeballs propped open as Walter droned on.

At last, I was put out of my misery when the president of the alumni association, Peggy Chapman, stepped up to the mike. Peggy had been one of those terminally perky kids in high school, the kind of kid who showed up at every pep rally, brimming with school spirit and, I suspect, just a few amphetamines.

After a highly fictional speech about our golden years at Hermosa High, she gave a moving tribute to Principal Seawright, seated at one of the ringside tables. Then door prizes were awarded—as well as a special prize to the person who'd traveled the farthest to come to the reunion.

"Linda Ruckle," Peggy announced, "flew in all the way from London, on her corporate jet. In case you guys didn't know it, Linda is chairman and CEO of her own cosmetics company. C'mon up, Linda, and get your prize."

And then the attractive blonde I'd seen talking with Dylan stood up. She strode to the mike in a nosebleed expensive cocktail dress, the picture of poise and grace. Was that Linda Ruckle, the same acne-ridden outcast from my gym class? If only Patti could see her now!

I guess the meek really could inherit, if not the earth, at least a corporate jet. And, from the way I'd seen them chatting together, what should've been my dinner date with Dylan.

The official ceremonies having come to a close, the band started up again, and Walter begged me for a dance.

"Please, Jaine," he pleaded. "Just one, before you go."

The combo was playing a slow tune. I figured my odds of being hurled across the room were minimal.

"Okay," I said, "but no dipping, no spinning, no twirling. No fancy moves of any kind."

"I promise. No fancy steps."

He guided me in an uneventful foxtrot, and as we shuffled around I couldn't help but feel proud of myself. I'd made amends for setting Walter's toupee on fire and for showing up with another guy at the prom. I'd atoned for my sins and could now head off into the world a guilt-free woman.

Yes, I had paid my dues, and I was just about to call it a night when Walter looked into my eyes and said:

"So how about it, Jaine? Will you give me a chance? Will you go out with me again?"

No, absolutely not. I had to end this thing here and now. I could not let him guilt me into one more date.

"I'm sorry, Walter. But it's not going to work for us."

"Oh." His Adam's apple bobbed as he gulped back his disappointment.

I felt like heel of the year, but I couldn't weaken, otherwise I'd still be dating this guy when I was on Medicare.

"There are lots of other women out there, Walter. And I'm sure one day you're going to meet someone special to have a relationship with."

"Oh," he said, "I already have. Min Lin."

"Min Lin?"

"My mail order bride from the Philippines. I haven't exactly met her yet, but in her picture she's really hot. We're getting married next month in Vegas."

"Wait a minute," I squawked. "You're getting married next month and you want to have a relationship with me?"

"Oh no, Jaine. I don't want to have a relationship with you. I want to have an *affair* with you! What Min Lin doesn't know won't hurt her. Wink wink, nudge nudge."

Can you believe the colossal nerve of that guy? I came *this-close* to nudge nudging him in his privates. Instead I took the high road and stomped off in righteous indignation.

And that's where fate stepped in and pulled one of her dirty tricks.

Because I hadn't stomped very far when I tripped over something. Something soft and furry and exceedingly slippery. Omigod! It was Walter's spare toupee! The damn thing must've slipped out of his pocket while we were dancing.

The more I tried to regain my balance, the more I stumbled, and before I knew it, I was reeling across the dance floor and heading straight for Principal Seawright.

Holy Moses! It was prom night all over again! All eyes were glued to my tush as I crash-landed in the poor man's lap.

The courtly octogenarian looked up at me with a wry smile.

"Ah, Ms. Austen," he said. "We meet again."

*　*　*

Any shards of dignity I'd had in high school had been scattered to the winds.

I leaped up from Principal Seawright's lap with a strangled cry and raced from the gym, my reputation as the Class Idiot cemented for all eternity.

Cursing myself for ever agreeing to go to the reunion, I sped all the way home, stopping only for red lights and an emergency pint of Rocky Road. I planned to eat it propped up in bed, hoping to calm my shattered nerves with chocolate and sitcom reruns.

Home at last, I trudged up the path to my apartment.

The minute I opened the door, I realized something was amiss.

The first thing I saw was Mamie's toy cell phone on floor. What was it doing here in the living room? Last I saw it, it was behind a firmly shut door in the bedroom.

The second thing I noticed was that the philodendron plant on my bookshelf was no longer on my bookshelf. It was on the floor, dirt splattered everywhere, its pot shattered to smithereens.

"Prozac!" I called out. But she was nowhere in sight.

Filled with misgivings, I headed down the hallway to the bedroom and saw the door wide open. How the heck did that happen? Maybe I hadn't shut it securely enough and Prozac had managed to push it open.

I stepped inside and gasped.

My bedroom looked like it had been struck by a cyclone. My pillows were on the floor, my shoes dragged out of the closet, and my hamper overturned, undies scattered about the room. And in a zany bit of interior design, my pajamas were draped over my lampshade.

And there on my bed, chewing happily on one of my favorite—and most expensive—suede boots, was Mamie.

Prozac was sprawled out on top of her, like Cleopatra lounging on the Nile, purring like a buzz saw.

I think I like having a dog.

"Mamie!" I shrieked, wrestling the boot away from her. "Did you do all this?"

At least she had the grace to look ashamed. Which is more than I can say for Prozac. She swished her tail delightedly.

Isn't she a hoot? She's so much more fun than I thought she'd be.

I surveyed the wreckage and sighed. I simply could not deal with it now. I'd clean up tomorrow. All I wanted was to get in bed with my Rocky Road and watch mindless TV.

Then, for the first time since I walked in the room, I noticed that the *Lassie* marathon that had been playing when I left was off the air. The television screen was filled with snow and static. Rats. The cable had gone out. I was just about to grab my phone and report the outage when I saw that the wire had been severed.

A few inches of cable still dangled from the back of the TV, but the rest of it lay coiled on the floor, cut clear through. Well, not exactly cut. Chewed was more like it. I could still see Mamie's teeth marks on the rubber.

"Mamie, you chewed right through my cable!"

Prozac leaped down from the bed and sniffed at the rubber.

What a neat trick, huh?

With a weary sigh, I plucked my pajamas from the lampshade and got undressed. Then I climbed into bed and scarfed down my Rocky Road listening to talk radio, where only the world's looniest nutcases can be found calling in on a Saturday night. One guy claimed he'd just been released by aliens from the planet Playtex.

"You think you had it rough, buddy?" I muttered. "Try going out with Walter Barnhardt."

When I'd licked every morsel of ice cream from the carton, I turned off the light and settled down for the night. Yes, I know I didn't brush or floss, but I was in no mood for oral hygiene.

I was just about to drift off to a well-earned sleep when I realized I hadn't taken Mamie outside to do her business.

I staggered out of bed, muttering a string of unprintable curses, and reached for my Reeboks. I started to put them on but stopped when my big toe felt something warm and squishy. It looked Mamie had done her business after all.

Prozac preened proudly from her perch on my pillow.

I taught her how to do that!

YOU'VE GOT MAIL

To: Jausten
From: Shoptillyoudrop
Subject: Happy Ending

Well, Roberto's gone and we all had a marvelous time.
Once Daddy saw that my "lover" was a chubby, balding
man, he was as charming as could be. And your father can
be quite charming when he wants to be. Which is why I
married him, I suppose. I have to remind myself of that the
next time he's driving me up a wall.

As for Roberto, what can I say? Such a sweet man—it's
hard to believe how many years have passed since our
picnic on the Spanish Steps. Try to enjoy every minute of
your life, darling; it all goes by so quickly.

And the really good news is that Daddy was feeling so
guilty about abducting Signor Facciobene, he didn't even
put up a fight when I insisted he return his library book. He
brought it back, meek as a lamb, paid the fine, and Lydia
issued him a new library card.

Best of all, he's given up that ridiculous lawsuit, which is all
that matters.

Your very relieved,

Mom

To: Jausten
From: DaddyO
Subject: If At First You Don't Succeed, Sue, Sue Again

Guess what, honey? Roberto turned out to be a pretty nice guy. I suppose I overreacted a tad when I heard he was coming. After all, your mom is entitled to an innocent romance in her youth. Live and let live. That's my motto.

Love and kisses,

Daddy

PS. I've decided to drop the Pinkus case. But don't worry, Lambchop. All my legal training wont go to waste. I'm suing the city of Tampa for false arrest.

Chapter 23

An odd rattling noise woke me the next morning. Rubbing sleep from my eyes, I saw Mamie at my bedroom door, jumping up and turning the handle with her paws.

So that's how she opened it last night. Mystery solved.

I looked around at the disaster area formerly known as my bedroom and groaned. Oh, Lord. It would take hours to clean up this mess.

I pried myself out of bed, threw on some jeans and a T-shirt, and took Mamie for a brisk walk to ensure no more accidents in my Reeboks. Then I fed Thelma and Louise (as I was now calling them) their breakfast. The little darlings had worked up quite an appetite after their rampage last night, and they dove into their chow with gusto.

And, I must confess, so did I. I nuked myself some coffee and a cinnamon raisin bagel, slathered with cream cheese, which I ate at the computer, checking my e-mail.

So Daddy was going to sue the city for false arrest. While he was at it, maybe he could sue the people who made Walter Barnhardt's toupee for hamster abuse. I just hoped for Mom's sake that she wouldn't have to live with Hank Austen, Esq. for too much longer.

Having scarfed down every last raisin in my cinnamon raisin bagel, I could no longer delay the inevitable. I gritted my teeth and set out to clean the mess in my apartment.

As predicted, it took hours.

When I was through, I plopped down on the sofa and looked over at Mamie, who was hard at work scratching my baseboard.

Prozac, draped over the back of the sofa, eyed her approvingly.

You go, girl! Get as much paint off as you can!

I was quite fond of the little fluffball, but it was obvious I had to find her a new home and get her away from Prozac's evil influence. If I kept the two of them under the same roof, I wouldn't have a roof for very long.

But who would take her?

I tried calling Kandi—hoping to convince her that a pet in her life would be less trouble and more rewarding than a man—but she wasn't home.

So I got out my address book and called practically everyone I knew, making my pooch pitch. But sad to say, nobody wanted an adorable white dog with a designer wardrobe and a penchant for chewing cable wire.

I was just about to give Kandi another try when I thought of Dickie Potter.

Daphna hadn't wanted Mamie around because she brought back memories of Patti. But conversely, maybe Dickie *would* want her around to keep Patti's memory alive.

I fished out his phone number from my purse and gave him a call, then briefly told him of Mamie's plight.

"Daphna was going to send her to the pound?" he said. "That's terrible."

"I thought maybe you might want to take her—seeing as Patti loved her so much."

"Of course I'll take her. When can you bring her over?"

"Right now, if it's okay with you."

"Sure, come on by."

I hung up, elated.

"How do you like that, Mamie? I found you a home!"

She looked up from the baseboard as if she'd understood.

"I'll go get your stuff."

She followed me into the bedroom and watched as I took her Gucci suitcase from the closet and packed her things. At the last minute, I tossed in one of my suede boots.

"Something to remember me by," I said, bending down and kissing her soft fur. "I'm gonna miss you, dollface."

And I would.

I drove over to Dickie's, my heart aching for Mamie. I hated shuffling her from owner to owner like this.

I looked at her—perched on the passenger seat, her head out the window, lapping up the wind—and for a minute, I felt like turning around and driving back home. But I couldn't possibly keep Mamie and Prozac together, not if I wanted to preserve my sanity and my apartment.

Besides, Dickie Potter was a sweet guy. I felt certain Mamie would be happy with him.

And indeed, the minute Dickie came to the door, she was all over him, slobbering at his ankles. Clearly this dog had never met a tree or a human she hadn't liked.

"Hi, Mamie," he said, bending down to pet her. "How you doing, girl?"

Dickie was looking good that day—clear eyed and freshly shaven—a far cry from the disheveled wreck who'd come to the door on my last visit.

Mamie licked his face with gusto.

"Thanks so much for taking Mamie," I said.

"Thank *you*." He smiled up at me. "You're the one who's doing me the favor."

Mamie panted in delight as he scratched her behind her ears, her tail wagging at rocket speed. And as I watched them together, a big load lifted from my shoulders, confident I was doing the right thing.

I brought in the rest of Mamie's things from my car and offered to stay and help get her settled.

"Oh, that's all right," Dickie said. "I can handle it. You've done more than enough already. Patti would be very grateful if she knew how kind you've been."

At the mention of Patti, his eyes misted over.

"I guess I'd better be going then."

With a twinge of regret, I scooped Mamie up in my arms for one last hug. And it was then, just as I was burying my nose in her soft fur, that I happened to glance into Dickie's hall closet. The door was ajar, and I could see a white jacket hanging from an inside hook. And not just any white jacket. A white *chef's* jacket. Just like the one Veronica had been wearing in her shop.

My keen powers of perception led me to deduce that it was, in fact, Veronica's jacket. Mainly because I could see the name "Veronica" embroidered on the pocket.

What the heck was Veronica doing here? And why was she hiding?

I intended to find out.

"Thanks again for taking Mamie," I said.

"It's my pleasure." For the first time, I detected a hint of impatience behind his smile. He wanted to get rid of me.

I blew Mamie a kiss and headed out to my Corolla. Dickie stood in the doorway, waving as I drove away.

I waved back, a phony smile plastered on my face.

But I didn't drive very far, just to the next block. Then I got out and headed back to Dickie's house, where I crept across the lawn and crouched under one of the living room windows.

I peeked inside and stifled a gasp. Veronica was stretched out on Dickie's sofa, leafing through the latest issue of *Gourmet,* wearing nothing but a bra and panties.

There was no sign of Mamie—or Dickie, for that matter. But a few seconds later, he sauntered into the room.

"I put the dog in the den so she won't bother you."

I could hear the muffled sounds of Mamie whimpering in the background.

"I still don't see why you had to take her," Veronica pouted. "You know how much I hate dogs."

"Because now that Austen idiot will run around telling everyone how devoted I am to Patti's memory. No one will ever suspect the truth."

Who the heck was he calling an idiot? I stiffened with indignation under my *Cuckoo for Cocoa Puffs* T-shirt.

Dickie picked up Patti's picture from the end table, the one taken in the Secret Gazebo.

"I hate looking at this thing," he said, slapping it facedown on the table. "What a holy terror she was."

"I'll say," Veronica sighed.

"I deserve an Academy Award for my performance as The Loving Fiancé. Every time I kissed her, I closed my eyes and thought of you."

He snuggled next to Veronica on the sofa and lifted the magazine from her hands.

"But it all worked out in the end, didn't it?" he smiled. "We got the money, just like I said we would."

Then he leaned in to kiss her, a big steamy suctionfest of a kiss.

I blinked in amazement.

Good Lord. It was *Veronica*, not Patti, who Dickie fell in love with at the Hermosa High reunion. Veronica had made a point of telling me how Dickie had taken one look at Patti and gone gaga. What a crock. *She* was the one Dickie had fallen for. Hadn't she been seen by everyone talking to Dickie and Normalynne that night? By the time Patti showed up, Dickie had already taken the plunge.

Now as I watched her run her fingers through his hair, I flashed back to Dickie's tousled hair on my first visit to his bungalow. Maybe Veronica was there that day, too. Maybe that's why he was so reluctant to invite me in. Maybe his disheveled look was due not to grief but to frantic sex.

Poor Patti. Dickie never did love her. That misty-eyed shtick of his was just an act to get his hands on her money. He probably got her to name him beneficiary in her will. And then, once he knew he'd inherit everything, his lover and partner in crime took a break from her cooking duties and sabotaged the balcony. The woman Julio saw up on the balcony was Veronica!

"And don't worry about the mutt," Dickie murmured, when they finally came up for air. "I'll bring her to the pound when things settle down. In the meanwhile, everyone will think I'm Saint Dickie."

I heard another muted whimper.

Poor Mamie. I couldn't leave her there with a pair of killers.

So there I was, ducked under the window, wondering how the heck I was going to get Mamie out of the house, when suddenly I heard the tinkling strains of "The Mexican Hat Dance."

It was not, I'm sorry to report, coming from inside the bungalow. That idiotic tune was the ringer I'd chosen, in a momentary lapse of good taste, for my cell phone.

"Somebody's outside!" I heard Veronica saying. "I think it came from that window."

At that point I had a choice. I could do the sensible thing and run for my life. Or I could stay and try to rescue Mamie.

It was no contest. Good sense didn't stand a chance against a sweetheart like Mamie. I stood up and screeched "Mamie!" at the top of my lungs.

I had no idea what good that would do, given that Dickie had her stowed away in the den. So you can imagine my joy—and surprise—when she came bounding into the room. She must've pulled her old Jump-Up-and-Turn-the-Door-Handle escape trick.

What a clever dog!

"Here, Mamie!" I called to her.

And like a curly-haired bat out of hell, she charged across the room and out the window into my arms.

Veronica, who'd been gaping openmouthed throughout this daring canine escape, now regained her powers of speech.

"Damn it!" she cried. "It's Jaine. She probably heard everything."

And then, tearing a page from Mamie's book, I did my own impression of a flying mammal out of Hades and took off down the block.

"Stop her, Dickie!" Veronica shrieked.

The door banged open as Dickie came bolting out of the house in hot pursuit.

Now Dickie was a tall, rangy athletic guy, and I'm about as athletic as your average lawn ornament. So normally he would've caught up with me in a heartbeat. But lucky for me, he was barefoot. As I puffed toward my car, Mamie in my arms, I heard him yelp in pain. I turned and saw him clutching his foot, plucking out what I figured was a piece of glass.

Which was why I was able to make it to my car and drive off unscathed.

"Oh, Mamie," I said, my hands trembling on the steering wheel, "I'm so sorry for leaving you with those dreadful people."

But Mamie had already forgotten her ordeal and was busy sniffing for buried treasure in my purse.

She'd just dug out a priceless used Kleenex when I heard the strains of "The Mexican Hat Dance." I was afraid it might be Dickie, but when I flipped open my phone, I was relieved to see Kandi's number on the screen.

"Hey, Kandi," I said, putting her on the speaker.

"Jaine, where were you? I tried calling you a few minutes ago."

So she was the one who blew my cover.

"You'll never believe what happened," she moaned. "It's just awful."

"What's wrong?"

"I'm stranded in Minneapolis!"

"What??"

"Remember my air date? The guy I was meeting on the plane?"

Yes, indeed. I remembered her plan to fake a business meeting in Minneapolis in order to hook up with a perfect stranger. How could I forget such an idiotic idea?

"He never even showed. I flew all the way to Minneapolis for nothing. And we landed in the middle of a storm. They closed the airport. I could be stranded here for days."

I restrained myself from breaking into a rousing chorus of I-told-you-so's.

"All the decent hotels are booked. And now I'm stuck in the world's crummiest motel with nothing to wear, except for a Vikings sweatshirt I bought at the airport gift shop. I don't even have a toothbrush. What am I going to do?"

But before I could offer any words of wisdom, I heard a car roar up behind me. There, in my rearview mirror, was Dickie behind the wheel of his yellow VW.

"Hang in there, honey," I called out to Mamie as I hit the gas pedal.

"How can I hang in there," Kandi whined, "when I'm trapped in this godforsaken motel?"

"I wasn't talking to you. I was talking to the dog."

"What dog?"

"The dog who's eating my wallet."

And it's true. Mamie, oblivious to my sudden burst of speed, had fished my wallet out of my purse and was now digging into it as if it were a T-bone steak.

"Don't eat the MasterCard!" I shrieked.

"Jaine, don't tell me you got a dog? Don't you have enough aggravation with Prozac? And speaking of aggravation, you should see the towels in this joint. They look like they've been recycled from a car wash. Ugh!"

By now I was barreling along the streets of Santa Monica, Dickie hot on my tail.

"Kandi, I think I'm going to have to call you back—"

"And the guy at the front desk looks just like Norman Bates. Honestly, I don't know how I'm going to sleep a wink tonight."

"Oh, no!" I gasped, as I saw a red stop light looming ahead.

"At last," Kandi sniffed. "A little sympathy."

Up until then, I'd been taking my chances and ignoring stop signs. But this was a signal at a major intersection. I thought briefly about taking my life in my hands and running the red light. But I abandoned the idea when I saw a logjam of cars backed up in front of me. I was trapped!

I checked my rearview mirror and saw Dickie pulling up behind me.

Damn.

He got out of his VW and started for my car.

Double damn. What if he had a gun? What if he pulled it on me and made me drive back to his place at gunpoint?

At the fringes of my consciousness I could hear Kandi whining about how there was nothing decent to eat in the motel's vending machine.

By now Dickie had reached my passenger door. I had to do something. And fast.

The light up ahead turned green, but the cars directly in front of me still weren't moving. So I did what any rational human being would do under similar circumstances:

I made a U-ey into oncoming traffic.

All around me drivers honked their horns and slammed on

their brakes. A medley of colorful curses wafted through the air. Thank heavens there wasn't a cop around or I'd be doing five to ten in traffic school.

As I drove off, I saw Dickie in my rearview mirror, shrugging in defeat. I also saw several motorists giving me the finger, but hey, I'd escaped Dickie and that's all that mattered.

"Are you okay, sweetie?" I said to Mamie, who was looking up at me, wide-eyed.

"Of course, I'm not okay," Kandi's voice squawked from my phone. "I've just spent the past ten minutes telling you how miserable I am. Oh, well. I suppose I'll survive. So what about you, hon? Anything exciting happening in your life?"

"Yes," I said, mopping the sweat from my brow, "I guess you could say things have been a little hectic around here."

Chapter 24

After that heart-stopping little adventure, I wanted nothing more than to go home and soak in the tub for the next 48 hours. But I could not allow myself that luxury. I had to find out if Patti had indeed named Dickie beneficiary in her will.

I figured the Devanes would probably know. So after a pit stop at McDonald's for some burgers—paid for with a credit card still damp with dog spit—I headed off to Bel Air.

I parked the Corolla in a shady spot on the Devanes' driveway and cracked the windows open so Mamie would have some air. Then I left her happily munching on her burger.

I only hoped Daphna wouldn't spot her and have a hissy fit.

But as it turned out, Daphna wasn't home. Apparently her period of mourning had come to an end.

"She's off in Beverly Hills on a shopping spree," Rosa told me when she came to the door.

Fortunately Conrad was home and agreed to see me.

"Poor Mr. Devane," Rosa said with a sigh, as she led the way to his study. "He's worse than ever. I've never seen a man so unhappy."

And indeed Conrad seemed in terrible shape. Worse, even, than when Patti first died.

He sat slumped at his desk, his eyes bloodshot, his hair

matted, a glass of scotch at his elbow. What a difference from the day I first saw him stepping out of his Rolls in his megabucks suit, his hair styled to perfection.

"So how can I help you, Jaine?" he asked after Rosa had left the room.

"I know you'll find this hard to believe, Mr. Devane, but I think Dickie Potter masterminded a plot to kill Patti for her money."

"Dickie?" He blinked, puzzled. "But Julio saw a woman on the balcony."

"He did. Veronica Hubbard was the one who did the dirty deed, but she was taking orders from Dickie. They're having an affair, you know."

If I expected him to be shocked, I was in for a surprise. There was nothing. Nada. No reaction whatsoever. He just took a slug of his scotch and stared at me dully.

"Look, Mr. Devane," I said, as gently as I could, "before I can go to the police, I need to know: Did Patti change her will to leave Dickie all her money?"

"Patti didn't have a will."

"No will? With all that money?"

"She refused to have one drawn up. She said they were 'spooky.' "

And just like that, my brilliant theory was shot to hell. Without a will naming Dickie her beneficiary, Dickie wouldn't have inherited a cent.

"I guess I'm wrong," I sighed. "If Dickie wanted to kill Patti for her money, he would've waited till after the ceremony."

"Oh, but he didn't have to wait," Conrad said with a bitter laugh. "The day of the wedding, he and Patti were already married."

Talk about your jawdroppers.

"Already married?"

"I just spoke with my attorney," he nodded. "It seems they

ran off to Vegas weeks earlier and got married in a quickie ceremony on the strip. Which meant Dickie inherited everything.

"Scheming sonofabitch," he muttered, downing the last of his scotch. "I should've known he was up to no good when I saw him kissing Veronica."

"You saw them kissing?"

"The day before the wedding. They snuck away from the cocktail party. I looked down at the gazebo and there they were, going at it like rabbits."

"Damn," he said, staring down into his now-empty glass, "I need a refill."

He heaved himself up from his chair and started for the door.

"Can I get you anything while I'm gone?"

"No, I'm fine."

Which, of course, was a gross exaggeration. I was far from fine. I was stunned, flabbergasted, totally blown away by what Conrad had just told me. Not that Patti had run off to Vegas, or that she'd gone through with the wedding in L.A. even though she'd already tied the knot. If I knew Patti, she did it to cash in on the gifts.

What stunned me was that Conrad would let Patti marry a man he knew was cheating on her. At the time, he had no idea Patti was already married. And yet he allowed her to go ahead with the wedding, in spite of the fact that he'd seen Dickie kissing another woman in the gazebo.

And that's when it hit me. The full significance of what Conrad had just said.

He said he'd *looked down* at the gazebo.

Patti told me that it was called the Secret Gazebo because it was hidden from view by the surrounding trees, visible only from her balcony. Which meant that Conrad Devane had to have been up on the balcony when he saw Dickie and Veronica kissing. And which also meant he was up there during the cocktail party, when the murderer jimmied with the railing.

You see where I'm going with all of this, don't you?

Conrad Devane could very well be the killer!

But he couldn't be. Julio swore it was a woman he saw out on the balcony. Had Julio been lying? And if so, why?

My mind spinning, I got up and paced the room.

It was a spacious book-lined study, with volumes no doubt purchased by the yard to color coordinate with the walls. Off to one side was a full-scale model of what I assumed was Conrad's latest housing development, Sunset Estates.

I glanced down at the meandering streets. They were lined with papier-mâché trees and miniature mansions and had names like Pleasant Drive, Leisure Lane, and Easy Street—

Whoa! *Easy Street?*

Didn't Julio tell his Godzilla apartment manager that he was going to be on easy street?

Was it possible he'd meant it literally?

What if it was *Conrad* Julio had seen on the balcony? What if Conrad made a deal with Julio? He'd give his gardener big bucks to keep quiet and swear it was a woman he'd spotted at the scene of the crime. Then he arranged to meet Julio on Easy Street, and when poor Julio showed up, instead of getting his payoff he got a bullet in his gut.

Oh, Lord. It all made sense.

Conrad was the killer!

I had to get out of there, and fast.

I raced to the door and flung it open, only to find Conrad standing there with a handgun aimed straight at my heart.

"So you figured it out, huh?" he said, shoving me back in the room with the muzzle of his gun. "The minute the words were out of my mouth, I realized I shouldn't have told you about looking down at the gazebo."

I tried to look as if I had no idea what he was talking about.

"Figured what out?"

"Oh, come on. You know it was me up there on the balcony. Why else would you be running out of my study like a chicken with her head cut off?"

"I honestly have no idea what you're talking about. I just remembered an important appointment, that's all. Now I really have to be going or I'll be late for my tonsillectomy."

"I'm sorry, my dear," he said, "but the only place you're going is to your final reward."

Oh, gulp. I didn't like the sound of that.

"But I don't understand," I said, abandoning the innocent act he clearly wasn't buying. "I thought you liked Patti."

"Oh, I did. Very much. But the sad fact is, I needed her money."

"You? But you're one of the richest men in Los Angeles."

"Make that past tense, sweetheart. *Was* one of the richest men. Due to a string of unfortunate investments, I'm afraid I'm in dire financial straights. I've already worked my way through my money—and Daphna's, too, for that matter.

"Fact is, I'm stone-cold broke. I needed Patti's money to finance Sunset Estates and get back on top again.

"If Patti died as a single woman," he said, plucking a piece of dust from one of the miniature houses on Leisure Lane, "her money reverted back to Daphna. Which meant it reverted back to me since I handle all of Daphna's finances.

"So I had to kill her, quickly, before she married Dickie." He actually managed to looked pained. "I hated to do it, but surely you can understand. I had no other alternative."

The man had no idea he was a roaring sociopath.

He adjusted one of the trees on Easy Street, clearly in love with the project he'd already killed twice for.

"It was simple enough to slip out during the cocktail party and jimmy the railing. I'd already snatched one of the workmen's drills and hidden it in the linen closet. That thing was powerful. Loosened the bolts in no time. Afterward I tossed the drill in the bushes, but I kept the drill bit. I figured I'd plant it on Cheryl and frame her for the murder. Everyone knew she loathed Patti. But when Normalynne showed up at the wedding and made such a scene, I decided to plant it on her instead."

"Let me guess. You dropped it in the backseat when you and Kyle ushered her out to her car."

"Clever touch, wasn't it? But it was all for nothing. What I didn't know at the time, of course, was that Patti and Dickie were already married. Dickie's the one who inherits, not me.

"What a waste of lives," he sighed. "First, Patti. Then Julio. And now you.

"Well, time to get started," he said, checking his watch. "Rosa should be gone by now. I sent her off on an errand. She won't be back for hours. Can't have any witnesses to your untimely demise, can we?

"Come on, honey." He nudged me with the butt of his gun. "We're going to take a little walk."

"Where to? Easy Street?"

"Ah, so you figured that one out, too. No, we're not going to Easy Street. We're going upstairs to the balcony. Back to the scene of the crime."

He shoved me out to the foyer, his gun lodged firmly in my back.

"Let's go," he said when we reached the foot of the winding staircase. "Upsy daisy."

With pounding heart, I started up the stairs. By the time we reached the top, I felt like I'd climbed Mt. Everest.

Conrad prodded me down the corridor to Patti's room, his gun now an appendage to my spine.

Patti's bubblegum pink palace hadn't been touched since the last time I saw it. Beyond the French doors, the balcony still loomed ominously, without a railing.

"Now here's what's going to happen," Conrad said. "There's going to be an accident. I'll tell everyone you came to the house investigating Patti's death and asked if you could search her bedroom for clues. I let you go upstairs alone. I warned you to be careful, that there was no railing on the balcony, but minutes later I heard you scream and came racing up the stairs only to find your mangled body splattered on the ground below. Now all you have to do, my dear, is jump."

"What if I won't?"

"Then I revert to plan B."

"I don't suppose that involves letting me go and forgetting we ever had this little chat?"

"Not exactly. Plan B is where I shove you in the trunk of my car and drive you to a deserted ravine and blow your brains out execution style."

"Ah. Death a la Julio."

"What's it going to be, sweetheart?"

So there I was, trying to choose between a suicide leap or a bullet to the skull, when suddenly a barking ball of white ball of fur came flying into the room.

Holy Mackerel. It was Mamie!

Somehow she'd managed to open the car door. What an escape artist. I swear, that dog was a regular Houdini with paws. I had no idea how she got into the house; probably through her old doggie door in the kitchen. I didn't care how she did it. All that mattered was that she'd distracted Conrad.

And indeed she had.

He'd whirled around in surprise when she made her grand entrance. Which meant that I no longer had a lethal weapon pointed at my internal organs. I took advantage of my momentary freedom to lunge at Conrad and tackle him from behind.

We spent the next few minutes grappling for the gun, Mamie nipping at Conrad's ankles. It wasn't long before the gun went off with a ghastly bang, shattering Patti's vanity mirror. Mamie, frightened, skittered under the bed. I only wished I could join her.

Finally, after taking an energetic bite of his wrist, I got Conrad to drop the gun. Whooping in triumph, I reached down to grab it.

Big mistake.

I'd given him the chance to tackle me. And he took it.

For a guy in his sixties he was amazingly strong. And as you well know, for a gal in my thirties, I was amazingly out of shape. Which is why seconds later, he had me pinned to the floor, his hands around my neck in a viselike grip.

Apparently he'd had a change of plan. Instead of shooting me, he'd decided to choke me to death. And he was doing a heck of a good job. I was gasping for air, certain that each breath was my last, when I heard:

"What the hell is going on here?"

Daphna stood in the doorway, aghast.

Conrad loosened his grip on my neck, and the minute he did, I started babbling.

"Daphna," I shrieked, my voice raspy from near-strangulation. "Thank God you're here! Your husband killed Patti! He did it for her money. He sabotaged the railing and put the drill bit in Normalynne's backseat and killed Julio on Easy Street and I discovered the truth, and now he's trying to kill me, too!"

"Don't listen to her, Daphna," Conrad said calmly, getting up from where he'd been straddling my chest. "*She* was try-ing to kill *me*. The woman is mentally unhinged. You can hear it in her voice."

Oh, rats. I had been ranting like a refuge from a loony bin, hadn't I?

"She's the one who killed Patti," Conrad continued, Mr. Cool and Collected. "She's had a pathological resentment toward her ever since high school. All her life she's been waiting for an opportunity to kill her, and when she was invited to the wedding, she finally got her chance."

"That's not true!" I wailed, once again sounding like a woman in serious need of her meds.

"Daphna, darling. We can't depend on the courts to deliver justice. We've got to take the law in our own hands and kill her ourselves."

Daphna's eyes narrowed into angry slits. She bent down and picked up the gun.

Oh, Lord. She believed him.

"Go ahead!" he urged. "Shoot her!"

But much to my surprise, she aimed the gun at Conrad.

"Shut up, Conrad," she said. "I know you're broke. When I went shopping today, all my credit cards were denied. I just got back from our lying, cheating dirtbag of an accountant who admitted under threat of a lawsuit that for years he's been allowing you to steal my money. According to him, we don't have a pot to piss in."

A nervous smile flitted across his face.

"So we're broke. No problem, darling. I'll get back on top again. But that doesn't mean I killed Patti."

"But he did!" I screeched. "He stole the workman's drill and snuck upstairs during the cocktail party and—"

"Enough, Jaine," Daphna said, holding up her hand. "You had me at *Thank God you're here.*"

She turned to Conrad, her eyes now blazing with fury.

"You killed my daughter."

"Okay, I killed her," he admitted. "But she was a brat. You said so yourself many times. You didn't even like her."

"She was my daughter, Conrad. I may not have liked her, but I *loved* her."

A fat tear rolled down her granite cheek.

"Call the cops, Jaine."

I did, and with the kind of lightning response you get in

places like Bel Air, they were at the front door in mere minutes. Mamie came out from hiding to give them a thorough sniffing.

Valiantly ignoring the dog saliva on their ankles, they took down our statements and, without further ado, hauled Conrad off to a luxury suite at the county jail.

When everyone finally cleared out, Daphna turned to me and started to speak.

"Jaine . . ." she began.

Was it my imagination or had that granite face somehow softened? Was there a spark of newfound compassion in her eyes? Maybe after all that had happened, she'd opened her heart and become a kinder, gentler Daphna. Maybe some good had actually come of Patti's death.

"Yes?" I said, flashing her an encouraging smile.

"Get that yapping mutt out of here."

Oh, well. I guess the only good to come of Patti's death was the deli at the funeral reception.

And Mamie, of course.

I scooped the little bitch in my arms and left the big one to her own devices.

Epilogue

Thanks to my testimony—and Daphna's—Conrad was convicted of first-degree murder and is now serving a life sentence at Homicide Estates, otherwise known as San Quentin Prison.

Needless to say, Daphna divorced him. Forced to take a job in the men's department at Saks, she promptly sunk her teeth into a billionaire Saudi oil magnate who divorced his three wives to make her his one and only. Last I heard, she was getting her Botox shots at a palace in Dubai.

And it turns out Conrad wasn't the only one on the brink of poverty. When Dickie tried to cash in on his inheritance, he discovered Patti had frittered away most of her father's money on her failed business ventures. Her line of doggie clothes alone cost over a million dollars.

Of course, Dickie and Veronica had never been planning to kill Patti. All they wanted was to walk away with a small fortune in a divorce settlement. And as soon as Veronica realized there were no big bucks on Dickie's horizon, she dumped him faster than a hot potato puff.

At which point, Eleanor Potter sprang into action and begged Normalynne to take Dickie back. Despite all evidence to the contrary, Eleanor still thinks Dickie is a prince among men.

But Normalynne, I am happy to report, is back at her old

job teaching high school biology and engaged to be married. To, of all people, one of her arresting officers! That's right. The brawny cop with the gentle voice. Apparently he fell in love with her the minute he first handcuffed her.

More good news. Patti's death seems to have been a turning point for Cheryl. She joined a twelve-step program and, after reading about Linda Ruckle in the Hermosa High newsletter, she wrote her a letter of apology about being so nasty to her in gym class. They started a correspondence, which grew into a friendship, and the bottom line is that Cheryl is now L.A. district manager for Linda Ruckle Cosmetics.

Denise Gilbert won her race for city council in a landslide. Trust me, this is just the beginning. Someday that woman is going to be California's first topless cheerleader woman governor.

As for Walter Barnhardt, he had the nerve to send me an invitation to his wedding. I didn't go, of course. But I did send him a gift I knew he'd treasure—his Sexometer. It was worth every penny in shipping costs to get rid of the darn thing.

And remember my fiancé-for-hire Brad aka Fireman Brad aka Dr. Francois Cliquot? Well, the other day I turned on the TV and there he was on a soap opera, playing the part of Dr. Boyd Radcliff, internationally famed neurosurgeon! Does life imitate art, or what?

And now—drumroll, please—I've saved the best news for last:

Lance has adopted Mamie the Wonder Dog! This time, for keeps. In the few days Mamie lived with him, Lance had fallen head over heels in love with her and was miserable without her. Yearning for the patter of her little paws on his hardwood floor, he took her back and made Kevin get allergy shots.

The only teeny downside to this story is that Kevin wound

up dumping Lance for a guy he met in the allergist's waiting room.

So Lance is single again, but he doesn't seem to mind. He's deliriously in love with his new roommate. He keeps making noises about setting up a playdate for Mamie and Prozac, but in the interests of avoiding a possible nuclear holocaust, I've been dragging my heels on that one.

Well, gotta run. Her royal highness needs her belly rubbed. Catch you next time.

PS. I never did hear from Dylan Janovici, the adorable English professor. But guess who did call and ask me out for dinner? Principal Seawright! Apparently he was quite taken with me and my tush at our last encounter. Needless to say, I turned him down. I wasn't about to go out with a man old enough to be too old for my mother. Last I heard, he was dating a waitress at Hooters.